Lucile Marshall was absolutely terrified.

"The evil . . . the evil's been set free," she moaned.

Then, as abruptly as she'd lost her composure, Lucile regained it. She stood up straight, shaking free of Paige and Phoebe, and looked Maxwell Harrington III straight in the eye.

"You fool. You pompous, arrogant idiot," she said. Then her eyes rolled back in her head and, gracefully as a silk handkerchief, Lucile Marshall folded in a dead faint to the floor.

Charmed®

Published by Simon & Schuster

PICTURE
PERFECT

An original novel by Cameron Dokey

Based on the hit TV series created by

Constance M. Burge

SIMON SPOTLIGHT ENTERTAINMENT
New York   London   Toronto   Sydney

S|S|E

SIMON SPOTLIGHT ENTERTAINMENT
An imprint of Simon & Schuster Children's Publishing Division
1230 Avenue of the Americas, New York, New York 10020
® & © 2005 Spelling Television Inc. All Rights Reserved.
All rights reserved, including the right of reproduction in whole or in part in any form.
SIMON SPOTLIGHT ENTERTAINMENT and related logo are trademarks of Simon & Schuster, Inc.
Manufactured in the United States of America
First Edition 10 9 8 7 6 5 4 3 2 1
Library of Congress Control Number 2005925346
ISBN-13: 978-1-4169-0025-2
ISBN-10: 1-4169-0025-X

Prologue

At first there was only darkness.

No, that isn't right, *he thought.*

It was important to be precise, to be as accurate as one could in all things. Wasn't that what a brain was for? Was it not with thoughts that a man shaped and controlled his world? If he began with a falsehood, did he not betray himself?

There had been something before the darkness.

Before the darkness, the pain had come.

It was so great and astonishing a pain that he sometimes thought the greatest astonishment of all was that he had endured it and remained alive. It had struck him from out of nowhere, seizing both his body and his will in a grip as unbreakable as the strongest iron. He ought to know. He'd tried his best to break it. Tried and failed. Time after time.

And it had been beautiful. That had been the most terrible thing of all.

It had been filled with colors, that pain. So bright

1

and shining that they'd blinded him. Then the darkness had come. But not before the colors of the pain
had incapacitated him, wreaking their havoc along
each and every separate nerve ending in his body,
seeking them out, as if the pain itself had been sentient, as if it had possessed a mind and a will of its
own.

Then as swiftly as it had struck, the pain released
him. His mind had floated in the dark void. He had no
idea how long he was there. But when he finally began
to awaken, to feel his mind at work again, he discovered that the colors had returned. Painlessly now, they
surrounded him. Though he'd soon discovered they'd
lost none of their ability to cause him harm.

He was trapped within them. The colors were a
glorious spiderweb and he the unfortunate fly. No
matter how he struggled, how he railed against his
fate, he could not break free. An entirely new version
of living hell. He still didn't understand how he had-
n't lost his mind.

But he hadn't. And, slowly, something new had
happened. Something entirely unexpected.

He'd begun to hope.

His enemies had not defeated him. He might be
down, but he was far from out. Someday he would be
released from his prison. Until then, he still had his
mind, and his mind was strong.

Strong enough to save him in the first place. Strong
enough to keep him alive. But he saw his error now,
understood the way that they had ensnared him. Knew
the part of him they'd taken and used against him.

He'd been impatient, too eager to work his own will. But in the darkness, he had time—time they had given him by trapping him in this beautiful and terrible place. Time he would use, to his own advantage this time.

And so he'd schooled himself to wait, the fly within the spider's web, spinning out his own web with each and every hour that went by. And the pattern was always the same, though the variations were endless.

No matter how long it took, how long he had to wait, he would find the way to make them pay for what they'd done. By the time he was finished, none of them would be left alive.

Chapter One

"Okay," Paige Matthews said. "This is going to be a problem."

From her position in the middle of the living room at Halliwell Manor, the big San Francisco Victorian that was home to the extended Halliwell-Matthews clan, Phoebe Halliwell turned around. Paige, who was her younger half sister, was standing in the doorway, hands on hips.

"You have a problem?" Phoebe said. "*Now?*"

"Absolutely." Paige nodded emphatically. "A really, really big one."

Phoebe stifled a sigh. Much as she wanted to support Paige, she could have had better timing. They had a gala to attend, and Phoebe already had excited butterflies in her stomach.

Buying herself a moment, Phoebe plucked a black silk shawl from the back of the couch and draped it around her bare shoulders. The silver paisley design embroidered on the shawl's surface shimmered in the light, the perfect foil for Phoebe's black evening gown. Tight-fitting halter top. Long, floaty skirt. The truth was, Phoebe Halliwell was dressed to the nines.

Her destination—and Paige's, too, for that matter—was the gala event to celebrate the reopening of the Lancaster Building, a San Francisco landmark. Built in the late 1920s as a sort of experimental artists' colony, the building had been damaged during recent earthquakes. A major citywide effort had successfully raised funds for its preservation. After months of work, it was now completely restored.

Although officially named after its architect, William Lancaster, the name "Lancaster Building" had never really stuck. Instead, in reference to the building's most outstanding feature, the life-size murals that adorned many of its external and internal walls, the locals had given the building the obvious nickname. They called it, simply, Mural House.

Phoebe had been preparing for weeks to attend the gala. The *Bay Mirror*, for which she wrote her weekly column, "Ask Phoebe," was a major sponsor. Her work had earned Phoebe highly coveted tickets to the event. Paige was accompanying her. Phoebe had thought Paige was as excited about the whole thing as she was. Up until about two minutes ago.

"Okay, what's the problem?" she asked.

"You are," Paige replied.

"Me?" Phoebe exclaimed, giving Paige her full and undivided attention at last. "What? How? Why?"

"You're too gorgeous," Paige said simply as she came all the way into the room. "How am I supposed to attract the handsome young scion of a wealthy San Francisco family, one who will be eager to cater to my every whim, with you walking around looking like that? The whole situation is completely unfair. I may have to stay home."

"You can't stay home. You're my date," Phoebe protested. "Okay, wait a minute. You want to attract a *what*?"

"Pay no attention to the woman in white with her fifty-cent words," Piper, the oldest of the three sisters, advised as she entered the room carrying her young son, Wyatt. Unlike her younger sisters, Piper was dressed functionally in an oversize white button-down shirt topping a slinky black skirt. A pair of sensible yet stylish shoes completed her practical, attractive outfit.

"It's hard to ignore her, especially when she's claiming I'm a problem," Phoebe answered.

Wrestling one of Wyatt's active arms into a sleeve, Piper looked up, her gaze traveling between her two younger siblings. "She is? I mean, you are?"

"Well, look at her," Paige said. "So aloof and elegant. That's a look that rich guys totally go for. It makes them feel secure. Like the girl's not after them for their money."

"I'm not after them for their money," Phoebe said. "I'm not after them at all. Why are we talking about rich guys, all of a sudden?"

"Because my mama always said it's just as easy to marry a rich man as a poor one," Paige replied.

"First of all, when did you start referring to your mother as 'my mama,' and second, when did you start shopping for a husband?" Piper asked.

"A girl's gotta keep her options open," Paige explained. "Especially when she's going to be surrounded by rich, eligible bachelors."

Phoebe rolled her eyes. Piper could tell her youngest sister was in one of her more whimsical moods, yet something still seemed to be bothering her. "It's not about guys, Paige. Come on, spill."

"Okay, here's the thing. I totally loved this dress when I bought it. Now, all of a sudden, I'm not so sure. Phoebe looks so understated and elegant. You don't think this is, I don't know, too over the top?"

With Wyatt safely ensconced in his sweatshirt, Piper settled him onto her shoulder and moved to stand at Phoebe's side. Together they regarded their youngest sister. Her evening dress was nothing like Phoebe's. In the first place, it was white, sleek, and body-hugging.

Ending just above the knee, it was completely covered with sparkling bugle beads. They caught the eye even when Paige was standing still. To set them dancing, all she had to do was breathe.

"Paige, I'm going to be completely honest with you," Piper said, her tone dead serious. "You're right to be worried—you're just a little confused on what to worry about. Every guy in the room's going to want to know who you are in that dress."

Paige laughed, an act that set the beads of her dress to career wildly. From his position in Piper's arms, Wyatt gave a sudden crow.

"There," Piper said. "You see? Even really young guys approve."

"He's facing the other way, Piper," Paige observed.

"Actually, in Wyatt's case, that may not make a difference," Phoebe commented, and was rewarded by Paige's smile.

"Thanks, you guys," Paige said as she moved to stand beside her sisters.

The three of them shared a smile. Though they all had very different personalities, and different ways of problem solving, they were always united by one simple thing: their love for one another. A love that took many forms. Not the least of which was their dedication to working as a team. Together, they were the world's most powerful witches, the Charmed Ones.

"So," Phoebe said briskly. "Now that that little crisis has been averted, what do you say we get this show on the road?" She began to move toward Halliwell Manor's entry hall, her shawl wafting out behind her.

"When it comes to guy hunting, Paige, I'll thank you to remember that I'm working tonight," Phoebe called back over her shoulder. "The newspaper was a big sponsor of the renovation. Any socializing I do is strictly professional. Personally, the person I want to meet most is Lucile Marshall."

"That's Isabella's daughter, right?" Paige inquired as she donned her evening wrap and followed Phoebe and Piper down the hall.

"Right," Phoebe nodded.

Isabella Marshall had been the driving force behind Mural House, as well as one of its most celebrated artists. When her marriage to an East Coast banker turned sour, Isabella had taken a bold step for a woman in the early part of the twentieth century. She'd divorced her husband, resumed using her maiden name, and returned to San Francisco, the city where she'd grown up. Accompanied by her young daughter, Lucile, Isabella had initially settled back into her parents' opulent mansion. But she hadn't stayed there long.

Instead, inspired by artistic movements in England such as the groundbreaking Omega workshop in Bloomsbury, Isabella Marshall had set about realizing her lifelong dream: to forge a place where artists could both create and sell their work. Mural House had been the result. The main floor was devoted to a combination of intimate salons and larger, more formal galleries. Living quarters and studios occupied the top floors.

Not surprisingly, to make sure that the building accurately reflected her vision, Isabella had spent many hours with the architect, William Lancaster. It hadn't taken long for the two to fall passionately in love. But their relationship had proved to be a stormy one. Having been through one unsuccessful relationship, Isabella Marshall knew what she wanted the second time around: a partnership, one that would acknowledge her achievements as an artist. At first it seemed as though this was something William could easily provide.

But, over time, as Isabella's work began to overshadow his own, William became jealous and controlling. When Isabella tried to pull away, William seemed to go almost insane, becoming completely obsessed with the desire to control her.

What lifted the story above the commonplace was the fact that the couple had poured out their hurt and confusion in a series of extraordinary letters, carefully preserved by Isabella's daughter, Lucile. That and the fact that, not long after they'd been written, William had disappeared without a trace. What had become of him was a mystery that had never been solved.

When Phoebe had discovered the existence of the letters, she'd contacted Lucile, asking for permission to publish them in her column. She'd expected the older woman, who was one of San Francisco's most famous recluses, to say no, or to simply not respond at all.

But to Phoebe's surprise and delight, not only had Lucile responded to her request, she'd phoned Phoebe herself to give the proposal the green light. The result was that, more than eighty years after they'd been written, Isabella's and William's letters were being read once more.

Phoebe had used the letters, particularly Isabella's, as a launching point for her readers to share their own experiences with what contemporary psychologists might call "controlling partners." She was certain that the issues the letters had raised over eighty years ago would still strike a chord. It turned out that her instincts were dead-on. The response from her readers had been nothing short of overwhelming. Phoebe's desk had been covered in letters for weeks. It would take at least another month to run them all.

"Speaking of work," Piper said as Phoebe swung the front door open, "we're still picking up the babysitter, right? We'll swing by, pick up Mandy, then you guys can drop us off at the club."

"Right," Phoebe said, nodding.

In addition to being a wife, mother, and one third of the most powerful witch trio of all time, Piper also owned and managed P3, her own nightclub. Though she'd been trying to cut back on her hours ever since Wyatt's arrival, recent staff upheavals had left her shorthanded and required her to be at the club.

The fact that her husband, Leo, who was also the Charmed Ones' Whitelighter, had been called away on business for the Council of Elders—his supernatural bosses—wasn't helping Piper's schedule much. Leo'd been away on his current assignment for about a week, and Piper had no definitive answer to that age-old married question: Honey, what time will you be home?

Under ordinary circumstances, Piper would have simply left Wyatt and the babysitter at Halliwell Manor. Recently, however, a series of murders had begun to haunt the City by the Bay, making the circumstances far from ordinary. Almost a month had passed since the first death had occurred. In the weeks that followed, two more people had died. Though the San Francisco police department was working overtime, they still had little to go on.

Naturally, the Charmed Ones had done some investigating of their own. But even their results had been inconclusive. The truth was, they weren't any closer to solving things than the police were: a situation that they weren't pleased about. So, after some discussion, the sisters had decided to stick with a tried-and-true plan: safety in numbers. Rather than leaving Wyatt and his sitter, Mandy, alone at Halliwell Manor, they would accompany Piper to work and camp out in her office. It was only a temporary situation, but she'd done her best to make the small space comfortable for them. There was a portable TV for the babysitter, and a portable crib for Wyatt.

"I want you guys to be careful tonight, all right?" Piper reminded her sisters as they made their way down the front walk to the family vehicle. "No going anywhere alone. Not even outside for a breath of fresh air. There's still a killer out there. Don't forget."

"As if we could," Phoebe said as she punched the button on her keys that unlocked the SUV doors. "By the way, the same goes for you. No quick trips to the alley to take out the trash. And don't take a cab home. If we're not already at P3 by the time you're ready to leave, call me on my cell and we'll be right over."

"Okay," Piper said with a nod.

"I just wish we *knew* something," Paige commented. She held the passenger door of the SUV while Piper settled Wyatt into his car seat, then slid in beside him. "Anything."

"Well, we do," Phoebe said as she got into the driver's seat. She waited until Paige had closed the back passenger door, then made her way to the front of the car to climb in before she continued. "Sort of."

"Sort of, if you count not finding anything in the Book of Shadows."

"Well, it did help us rule some things out," Piper said. "We know whatever's doing the killing is definitely not a demon, or a warlock, though we still can't entirely rule out some sort of supernatural tie."

"That's not much help," Paige said glumly, as Phoebe started the car. "We just know what it isn't. But we don't know who, or what, it is."

"Oh, yes, we do," Phoebe said, her voice grim as she put the vehicle into reverse and backed smoothly out of the drive. "It's evil, even if we don't know yet what it looks like. No matter how long it takes, no matter what it takes, we're going to find the way to stop it."

Chapter Two

"Wow," Paige said, a short time later. "Now *that* is officially cool."

"For the record," Phoebe responded, "officially, I agree with you."

Though there was a steady stream of well-dressed partygoers entering Mural House's front door, Phoebe and Paige had chosen to linger for a moment out on the sidewalk. From there, they had a perfect view of the exterior of Mural House.

The building itself was tall and boxy. It actually looked a lot like a classic New York City brownstone, though it wasn't brown. Instead it was a soft gray, much like the fog that would so often creep in from the bay to envelop it.

But it wasn't the shape of the building that held Phoebe's and Paige's attention. It was what was painted on its exterior that had them spellbound. On the front of the building—on all sides of it, in fact—a series of vivid murals created the

15

details of what you might expect to find on a San Francisco street: a painted lady. An elegant, elaborately decorated Victorian.

"I just can't get over how real it looks," Paige commented. "I mean, I knew restoring the murals was going to make them more colorful, but I never expected this."

"I know what you mean," Phoebe said, nodding.

The murals were so realistic, it was hard to tell the painted Victorian house from the real ones that surrounded it. Painted lace curtains seemed to flutter at windows. Painted flowers spilled from painted wrought-iron flower boxes. If Paige turned her head, then looked back again quickly, she could even swear she caught a glimpse of a face in an upstairs window.

Like other native San Franciscans, Paige had grown up with Mural House. It had been easy to take the building for granted. Over the years, the outside murals had faded. The building had fallen into genteel disrepair and had become nothing more than a quaint and quirky local landmark. But now that the murals had been restored to their former glory, it was easy to see the genius behind them.

"No two ways about it," Phoebe remarked, "Isabella Marshall was one hell of an artist."

"If the outside is this good, I can hardly wait to see what the inside looks like," Paige commented excitedly.

Arm in arm, the sisters sailed up the red carpet and through the open door of Mural House.

They are so beautiful, he thought.

From across the street, he watched them. The beautiful ones. A fascinating collection of San Francisco's elite—old money mingling with new. City officials rubbing elbows with artists, both established and up-and-coming. *And almost all of them dressed in black*, he couldn't help but notice. As if the building they were entering contained not a celebration of its own renewal, but the world's most elegant funeral.

Funeral. Now there was a word to make him smile.

He tried not to feel self-satisfied. Honestly, he did. But why not just admit it? Sometimes he had to admire the way his mind worked, conjuring up links and images all on its own. Because the truth was, there'd been a few funerals in San Francisco lately. More than a few, in fact. Events he knew a thing or two about.

I ought to, he thought, as his smile sharpened. *I'm the one responsible for them.*

In front of him, the crowd of onlookers milled and shifted, waiting for the next set of fashionable guests to arrive. Even as he allowed his body to move with the flow, he watched them through narrowed eyes. *I could ask any man or woman here*, he thought. *I could ask anyone.*

And each and every one of them would say

exactly the same thing: San Francisco had a problem. A big one.

There was a killer stalking its tree-lined streets. Creeping up its hills. Slithering across its cobblestones. A serial killer who had police frustrated and baffled, who had all but the most desperate off the streets, and who had everyday people making midnight runs to the hardware stores in search of extra-strength dead bolts to reinforce the locks on their doors. A killer who left no one feeling safe, not even the beautiful people at the gala tonight. A killer whose next move had, so far, proved to be entirely unpredictable, because his victims crossed social, racial, and economic lines.

As far as most people knew, there was just one way in which the killer was consistent: the death he brought to those he touched. Only the police knew the rest, the worst. The details were kept from the public, as was the policy for cases of this severity. No one but the police knew the truth: San Francisco didn't just have a serial killer, it had a trophy hunter. Each victim had been missing a body part. And not once had it ever been the same one.

A sudden, dazzling sweep of light played across his face as one of the searchlights brought in to help commemorate the opening of the San Francisco landmark known as Mural House shone its rotating beam along the street before once more taking to the skies. Startled, he lifted a hand to cover his face, then turned away.

That settled it. There were too many people here now. It was time to move on.

He was done, anyway. He'd seen what he needed to see. The building, restored to its former glory, looking as if it were dressed up to attend its own party. But most of all, the people. So beautiful. So full of life.

So full of fear. Even through the bright lights and the party clothes, he'd still seen that. The quick, furtive looks over well-dressed shoulders. Oh yes, the citizens of San Francisco were full of fear.

Just not quite full enough.

He moved off down the street, the crowd thinning around him.

"Hey, great golden oldie," a man said, catching the tune he hummed as he passed by.

"One of my favorites, for sure," he responded with a . smile. Then he was turning off the brightly lit street, walking into the gathering dark. With every step he took toward the darkness, he sang a little more loudly.

"Help me make it through the night. . . ."

Chapter Three

"Phoebe Halliwell?"

At the sound of her name, Phoebe turned, though the truth was that her mind was still on what was in front of, not behind, her. For the last fifteen minutes, at least, she'd totally ignored the festive party that completely filled the down-stairs rooms. Instead she'd been completely entranced by the largest of the interior murals in Mural House.

Covering one entire wall of what had once been the main salon where the artists-in-residence sold their work, the mural was in the style known as trompe l'oeil, a French term that described the style's best-known feature: its ability to fool the eye. It looked three-dimensional. It looked real. So real, in fact, that Phoebe was still having trouble convincing herself that the windows she was looking through, the lovely, lush gardens beyond them, were created in paint.

Adding to the mural's charm was the fact that there were cleverly designed "holes" made to be filled by actual three-dimensional objects. During Mural House's heyday, the items would have been those the artists wished to sell. Isabella Marshall's mural was therefore not only a magnificent work of art all on its own, it was designed to highlight the work of her fellow artists.

Behind her, Phoebe heard a dry chuckle, and she turned around.

"It's hard to look away, isn't it?" the person who had claimed her attention said. In front of Phoebe stood a small, elderly woman dressed in elegant evening black. Around her neck was one of the most magnificent ropes of pearls Phoebe had ever seen.

"In the evenings, when the salon was closed," the woman continued, stepping closer to the painting, "I used to sneak downstairs and spend hours trying to discover all the hidden images she said she'd tucked away, somewhere in the paint, just for me to find. Naturally, the first thing I discovered was that she'd put me in the garden."

Stepping to Phoebe's side, the woman gestured toward the mural, to the nearest painted window. Through it, Phoebe could see a lush green lawn. In one corner, almost out of the frame, she could just make out the edge of a blanket, and the ruffle of a dress out of which poked a young girl's shoe. A puppy had its nose nearby, as if considering taking a chomp of the shoe even while the owner's foot was still inside it.

"Lucile," Phoebe said delightedly as she turned back to her companion. "You're Lucile Marshall."

"None other," the older woman acknowledged. "You *are* Phoebe Halliwell, aren't you?"

"I am," Phoebe said. "And I'm delighted to meet you."

She held out a hand. Lucile Marshall smiled, the action sending her face into soft, papery wrinkles as she shook Phoebe's hand.

"And I you, my dear," she responded. "I've enjoyed our phone conversations, but I couldn't wait to meet you in person. I regret it wasn't possible until now. I don't get out much these days, I'm afraid."

Not just these days, Phoebe thought, though she kept the thought to herself. Even as a young woman, Lucile Marshall had been famously reclusive. Though her social standing had given her many opportunities to be in the public eye, Lucile had kept resolutely out of the limelight. So successfully had she done this, in fact, that there was hardly any public record of what she looked like. Until this moment, Phoebe'd had no clear idea of what to expect when she finally came face-to-face with Lucile Marshall.

Her mother, Isabella, had been tall and wiry, but Lucile reminded Phoebe of nothing so much

as an old-fashioned apple doll. Not that she was
dumpy; just small and soft and ever so slightly
round. But her voice was firm and clear, her
handshake strong. Her deep blue eyes held what
Phoebe was pretty sure was a mischievous
sparkle, layered over . . . something else.

Something secret, Phoebe thought suddenly.
Secret and dark. Could this be the reason Lucile
had chosen to remain hidden for so long? One
thing seemed crystal clear, though. Whatever
her reasons for keeping out of sight for so many
years might be, Lucile Marshall was just like her
mother's paintings: There was a great deal more
to her than met the eye.

"Thank you again for agreeing to let me publish your mother's letters," Phoebe said. "And
William Lancaster's, too, of course. The response
has just been overwhelming."

"I've been following your column," Lucile
said. A waiter with a tray of hors d'oeuvres
passed by. Without missing a beat, Lucile
reached out, snagged a caviar-laden canapé, and
popped it into her mouth. "You're right," she
continued after a moment. "The response has
been overwhelming. It's also been an enormous
disappointment."

Phoebe felt her spirits plummet abruptly.

"I'm sorry you feel that way," she said, striving to keep her tone even and calm. No matter
how personally let down she felt by Lucile's
reaction, Phoebe had to remember she was here

this evening as a representative of the paper, and she needed to keep her response professional. "I tried to show how relevant the issues in them were, even after so much time."

"And you did an excellent job," Lucile replied. "I'm not faulting you, my dear. Far from it. But don't you find it disappointing that, nearly eighty years after my mother's experiences, so many modern women should write letters of their own to say things haven't changed very much?"

"I never thought of it in quite that way," Phoebe answered, genuinely struck by Lucile's comment. "Put like that, I'd have to say you're absolutely right. It *is* disappointing; maybe even frightening."

As if as startled by Phoebe's response as Phoebe had been by Lucile's, the older woman looked straight up into Phoebe's eyes. For one split second, Phoebe could have sworn she saw the secret at the back of Lucile's eyes leap forward, as if straining to get out.

"'Frightening,'" Lucile echoed. "How very astute of you to say so, Miss Halliwell. I agree with you, as it happens. I hope you never need to know how much."

Before Phoebe could frame a way to ask what her companion meant, a second waiter appeared, this time bearing a tray of colorful drinks. Lucile turned aside to make her selection. By the time she'd turned back to Phoebe, the secret had been locked away once more. Lucile's eyes were a simple, sparkling blue.

How many people has Lucile fooled over the years with that look? Phoebe wondered.

"There now," Lucile said. "Chances are I've gone and said something I shouldn't have, and after I promised myself . . ."

Whatever else she'd been about to say was drowned out by a sudden voice, booming out over a microphone. "Your attention—may I have your attention, please, ladies and gentlemen?"

Of mutual accord, Phoebe and Lucile turned toward the sound.

"Oh, dear," Lucile Marshall said, though, privately, Phoebe thought the older woman was relieved by the interruption. When she saw who was at the microphone, however, Lucile began to frown in earnest. "Oh, dear," she said again, definitely sounding as if she meant it this time around.

"It would seem that, in spite of my best efforts, the moment I've been dreading all evening is about to arrive. That man—" She gestured to the distinguished man in a tux who was standing at the far end of the room behind a microphone.

"You mean Maxwell Harrington III, the head of the restoration committee?" Phoebe prompted.

"Harrington," Lucile said, pouncing on the name like a cat on a spider. "Yes, that sounds right. A ridiculous name, if you'll pardon my saying so. Not that it can be considered his fault, of course. But I've always thought it unspeakably arrogant and selfish to name one's child after oneself. And to do it generation after generation . . ." She made a disapproving click in her mouth. "Every individual should have his or her own name, a chance to develop his or her own identity, don't you think so, Miss Halliwell?"

"Phoebe," Phoebe said as she battled an impulse to smile. Whatever had prompted to Lucile to keep out of sight for so many years, it was plain she didn't do so because she was senile. Keeping up with her lightning-quick turns of mind was a full-time job.

"That Harrington the Third man insists on introducing me tonight," Lucile went on. "I tried to tell him I strongly preferred to remain anonymous. In fact, aside from my desire to meet you, I'd have been just as happy to stay home. I value my privacy very highly. And I don't like crowds. I find them . . . unsettling. That man ignored every single word I said. I might as well have been talking to a sentient form of steamroller."

Phoebe laughed before she could stop herself. There was just something about the way Lucile Marshall turned a phrase. As if inspired by this response, Lucile took a step closer and linked her arm through Phoebe's.

"Allow me to offer you some advice, my dear," she said, her tone confidential. "As you grow older, make every effort to be as outspoken and eccentric as possible. That way, people will find you unpredictable. Instead of ignoring your wishes, they'll find you terrifying even when you're not, and they'll toe the line."

"You think you're not terrifying?" Phoebe asked. In the next moment, she could feel the hot color rushing to her face. "Miss Marshall," she stammered. "I'm so sorry. Please let me apologize."

"You must call me Lucile. But as for apologizing, I'm afraid I simply can't allow it," Lucile Marshall answered smartly. Vaguely, Phoebe could hear Maxwell Harrington III begging the crowd for silence yet a second time. "Please don't be concerned," Lucile went on. "I'm not annoyed. Far from it. The truth is, I've always rather aspired to be considered terrifying."

"Ladies and gentlemen," Maxwell Harrington III's voice boomed out for the third time. At long last, the noise in the room subsided to a level that seemed to suit him. He cleared his throat and went on.

"On behalf of the restoration committee, it's my very great pleasure to welcome you all here to Mural House tonight. This is an important night for the city of San Francisco. A night for us all to be proud. Instead of allowing one of our most beloved landmarks to fade away, we've given her a new lease on life. If you ask me, she's the belle of the ball."

There was an enthusiastic round of applause.

"There are many people to thank this evening," Maxwell Harrington III continued. "I *could* stand up here and introduce them all."

A mock groan swept through the assembled guests, followed by a quick round of spontaneous laughter. Phoebe caught a glimpse of Paige's dress sparkling in the salon's overhead lights. She was standing by the waiter who'd just handed Lucile her drink. Paige was clearly listening to the speaker, but unless Phoebe was totally misreading her younger sister's body language, there was also a little flirting going on.

"Or, I could introduce the one person I believe everyone here would like to meet tonight. The person without whose permission none of the work on Mural House would have been possible. I refer, of course, to Miss Lucile Marshall." With his free hand, Maxwell Harrington III gestured toward the back of the room, at precisely the place where Phoebe and Lucile were standing.

It was like watching a school of fish, Phoebe thought. As if on cue, every single head in the room swiveled in their direction. Lucile's grip on Phoebe's arm tightened.

"Oh, dear," Lucile murmured once again. She pulled in a deep breath, as if steeling herself. "I'd forgotten what it was like," the older woman said, almost as if to herself. "All those eyes." She straightened her shoulders as if preparing to go into battle. "Still, I'd better make the best of it, I suppose."

She took a few steps forward, then came to a halt when Phoebe stayed right where she was. "Where do you think you're going?" Lucile whispered as the crowd began to open up before them like the parting of the Red Sea.

"I was thinking something along the lines of nowhere," Phoebe hissed back through teeth clenched in a smile.

"Think again," Lucile said. "You're the only person I know in the entire room, Miss Phoebe Halliwell. That makes you my only friend. Where I go, you go."

Lucile's eyes, bright and clear as water with treacherous shoals beneath, looked straight into Phoebe's own. In that moment, Phoebe thought she knew what Lucile Marshall's secret was: sorrow.

"Anything for a friend," Phoebe said, and had the pleasure, just for a moment, of seeing the darkness disappear entirely from Lucile Marshall's eyes.

"Thank you, my dear," Lucile said.

Together, the women made their way toward the microphone.

Chapter Four

"Uh-oh," Piper's head waitress, Donna Peterson, said. "Looks like trouble."

Behind the bar at P3, where she'd been pinch-hitting for most of the night, Piper looked up. Quickly, her keen eyes scanned the club. It didn't take long to spot the location that had provoked Donna's comment.

"Guy at table three?" she asked.

Donna nodded.

Though Saturday was always a busy night at P3, this Saturday night was particularly hopping. Often, if she had to bring Wyatt with her to work, Piper could sneak a minute or two to jet back to her office to take a quick break and check on how he and the babysitter were doing at the same time. Not tonight, though.

Tonight Piper had stayed on her feet, and she'd stayed on the floor. There was an edginess to the crowd that seemed unusual to her. An uneasiness, even a darkness. *They're afraid*, she realized. All over the city, even people who normally stayed home were making the effort to go out in public. Preferably to a place with very bright lights. If the crowd at P3 was anything to go by, attendance at restaurants and nightclubs was way up. But Piper would have been willing to bet that movie theater attendance was down.

No one wants to be alone, particularly not alone in the dark, she thought.

Personally, she didn't blame them one bit, even if it did make things more challenging at the club. Hadn't she and her sisters just been discussing the very same thing earlier that evening? Hadn't they altered their usual routines so that none of them would have to be alone?

But the knowledge that she, Phoebe, and Paige weren't the only ones feeling the pressure of the current situation in the city didn't make Piper feel any better. If anything, it made her feel worse. Much as she and her sisters might have in common with her P3 customers, Piper knew there was one way in which she wasn't like any of them at all.

She was a witch. She was one of the Charmed Ones.

As far as Piper was concerned, that meant she should be part of the solution, not part of the crowd. Unfortunately, considering the trouble she and her sisters had had in solving San Francisco's current grisly problem, Piper might as well be a member of the herd.

Moo, she thought.

"Lone wolf." Donna's voice jerked Piper back to the present.

"I'm sorry," she said. "What?"

"The guy at table three," Donna explained. With the ease of long years of practice, she placed her drink order, then leaned against the bar as she waited for what she'd ordered to come up. Piper helped by pouring out a glass of chardonnay.

"Prefers his whiskey straight, been at it pretty steadily all night," Donna went on. "Jennifer and I did a quick confab when he took his last bathroom break. If that boy can walk a straight line, I'm a trapeze artist."

"Okay," Piper said. She poured a second glass of wine, then placed it on the bartop beside Donna. "So it's definitely time to cut him off. You worried Jen can't handle things?"

Jennifer was Piper's most recent hire. She was quick and enthusiastic. Piper had pretty much liked her on the spot. So much, in fact, that she'd given Jennifer the job even though she didn't have all that much experience, which the younger woman had been completely up front about. Piper had liked both her potential and her style. With a little more time on the clock, Piper was positive Jennifer could handle whatever the customers threw her way. In the present circumstances, however . . .

"To tell you the truth, I'm not quite sure,"

Donna admitted as she began to place drinks in careful order onto her tray. "That's why I came to the big boss. My gut says he's going to be trouble." She gave a shrug. "Professional intuition—what can I tell you?"

"Professional intuition," Piper echoed, smiling even as she continued to assess what was happening across the room. "Good term. I like it. Suppose I go see what mine tells me?" Reaching behind her back, Piper began to untie the apron she'd donned to work behind the bar.

"You go, girl," Donna said.

"That's 'boss girl,'" Piper said, with a perfectly straight face. "How many times do I have to tell you?"

Donna chuckled. Flashing Piper a wicked grin, she picked up her tray and headed off into the crowd.

Sighing internally, Piper signaled the bartender that she was going to take a break, then stepped out from behind the counter. Swiftly but unobtrusively, she began to make her way toward the table the staff all knew as number three, checking out the situation as she went. Handling customers who couldn't handle themselves was a necessary— though hardly favorite—part of Piper's job.

As she approached the table, Piper could see the dynamic. Jennifer, the waitress, was standing on the far side of the table, facing in Piper's general direction, her face fixed in a determined smile. The guy at the table was speaking rapidly, his face flushed an angry red, a combination of anger and alcohol.

Score one for professional intuition, Piper thought.

Handling the lone wolf definitely looked like it could be a problem. Though, for her money, Piper would have said there was more grizzly bear than wolf in this guy's background. The descriptive terms "big" and "burly" didn't even begin to cover it. This was a guy who could do some serious damage if things got out of hand. A thing that made him not just trouble, but potentially big trouble.

"Piper Halliwell?"

"Yes?" Piper answered automatically. Her body halted, but her eyes remained fixed on what was happening at table three. Across the room, the grizzly bear had apparently decided it was time to demonstrate his abilities as a biped. He was starting to stand up.

"Gil Townsend," the voice that had caused Piper to halt went on. "Danny Logan over at Dockside mentioned you were looking for a manager. He said it would be okay if I just stopped by."

"I am, and it is," Piper said, responding to his statements in order, still without taking her eyes off what was happening on the club floor. "Just give me a minute to sort something out, will you? Make yourself comfortable up at the bar."

Her eyes fixed on the guy she was now mentally dubbing Mr. Grizzly, Piper hurried off.

"Excuse me, sir," she said, reaching the table just as Mr. Grizzly finally managed to lumber all the way to his feet. "I'm Piper Halliwell, the club owner. Is there a problem?"

At the sound of her voice, Mr. Grizzly swung around, an action that caused him to tilt dangerously to one side. He grabbed the back of his chair for support.

Oh, yeah, Piper thought as she made quick, approving eye contact with Jennifer in the time it took Mr. Grizzly's own bloodshot ones to locate her and focus. *This guy has definitely had enough.*

"You're damn right there's a problem," Mr. Grizzly growled. "She"—he jerked a finger over his shoulder in Jennifer's direction—"is trying to cut me off. I'm just sitting here, minding my own business. I'm not hurting anyone."

"At the moment, no, you're not," Piper agreed, careful to keep her voice pleasant and calm. "But, as I'm sure you're aware, the club has a legal responsibility to make sure the situation stays that way *after* you walk out of our doors. We have an obligation, to you and to others, to determine when it's time for you to stop consuming alcohol. I'm sorry if you disagree with the line we set, but I'm afraid it's a hard-and-fast one."

She summoned up a smile. "Now, why don't you let me call you a cab?" she went on, her tone upbeat but firm. "P3's treat."

Mr. Grizzly straightened and let go of the back of the chair. The expression on his face made Piper wish she could take a step back, but she held her ground.

"You're saying I don't know when I've had enough?"

"Of course not," Piper responded.

"Sure sounds that way to me. Sounds to me like you're like every other woman I've encountered. Opinionated and bossy. How'd you like me to show you what I think of your opinions?"

"Is there a problem?"

At the sound of a third voice, Piper jumped. She'd kept her attention so tightly focused on what was happening in front of her, she hadn't felt the newcomer move to stand at her side.

She did recognize the voice, though. Gil Townsend, the guy who'd stopped by about the manager position. *Either his timing is brilliant, or he's going to be the next one I boot out the door,* Piper thought.

"I'm Gil," Gil Townsend said, before Mr. Grizzly could recover from his own surprise at Gil's arrival. Gil took a step forward and held out his hand, as if genuinely happy to meet the irate mammal glowering before him. His action forced Mr. Grizzly to shift position slightly, so that now the three of them formed a sort of lopsided triangle. Piper could see both her customer's face and Gil Townsend's.

"Sorry, I'm afraid I didn't catch your name," Gil went on.

"Norman," the big man said. Piper bit down brutally on the inside of her lip to hold back an involuntary smile. Totally fascinated, she watched Norman watch his own hand swing up to meet Gil's. From the expression on his face, it was plain that shaking hands had been the last thing on Norman's mind. Still, there he was, doing it, for all the world as if his hand had suddenly developed a mind of its own.

"Nice meeting you, Norman," Gil said easily. He shot Piper a quick look. *Just go with me on this, will you?* it seemed to ask. *Give me a chance to show what I can do.* Piper hesitated a fraction of a second, then gave a barely perceptible nod. As a manager, handling difficult customers would definitely be a part of Gil's responsibilities. She might as well see how he handled this one.

"You want another drink?" Gil said now. "Am I getting this right?"

"Yeah," Norman answered, his tone aggrieved. "That's right. I'm just knocking back a few, minding my own business. That's all. Nothing wrong with that, is there?"

He glared at Piper. She gave him her sweetest smile.

"Of course not," Gil said easily. "But, just between you and me . . ." He paused, as if waiting for Norman's permission to continue the discussion, mano a mano. Not only that, he eased himself forward ever so slightly, as if to cut Piper out of the conversation altogether.

Piper felt a quick spurt of irritation shoot through her, then fought it down. *It is a clever move,* she thought. Much as she hated to admit it, there really were guys who simply could not deal with women in authority. It hadn't taken more than a couple of seconds for Piper to size Norman up as one of them, and it was pretty clear that Gil Townsend had as well. Piper might not like the feeling of being usurped, but Gil had asked for her permission to act, and as long as his actions had a favorable outcome for the club . . .

As if already anticipating his own positive outcome, Norman followed Gil's lead, stepping away from the table, angling his body away from Piper's. As he did so, Jennifer scooted around him to stand at Piper's side.

"See, the thing is . . . ," Gil began. Easily, he rested one hand on Norman's shoulder as he began to steer the big man toward the bar— closer to the source of the problem, the alcohol Piper was refusing to give him. It was also, Piper had to acknowledge, closer to the door.

"A real man knows his own limits, right? He doesn't want somebody else telling him that," Gil went on.

"Well, yeah," Norman said. "I mean, of course not. I was trying to explain—"

"So basically what we have here," Gil interrupted smoothly, "is a failure to communicate. You know you've had enough. You've just admitted it. What you don't need . . ." Almost out of earshot now, Gil cast a look back over his shoulder at Piper, as if to check on how he was doing. Again, Piper gave a small nod. He was good, she had to give him that.

"What we don't need," Gil went on, "is a bunch of . . ."

Fortunately—or unfortunately, Piper could't quite decide which—that was the moment at which Gil's voice became overwhelmed by the noise of the club. Though, if she'd had to place a bet, Piper would have put money on the fact that the next word out of Gil's mouth was "women." Or maybe even "uppity women."

Male bonding. It's a beautiful thing, she thought sarcastically.

"Wow," Jennifer said as she and Piper watched Gil and Norman make their way to the bar. The two men stood talking for a moment, looking for all the world like old pals. Then Gil pulled a cell phone from a shirt pocket, and Piper figured they were home free.

"I really thought we were in for it until Mr. Tall, Dark, and Smooth showed up," Jennifer went on. "How come you didn't tell anyone you'd hired a new manager?"

"Probably because I didn't know it myself," Piper answered with a smile.

But unless she very much missed her guess,

that was a thing that would change before the night was over.

"I haven't had the chance to thank you yet," Piper said a couple of hours later.

After the successful defusing of the Mr. Grizzly bomb, once more with Piper's permission, Gil had stayed until closing, helping out around the club. The cell phone call he'd placed had actually been to a local limousine company. Not only had Mr. Grizzly gone home without any additional fuss, he'd gone home in style, an aspect of the situation Gil had insisted on paying for himself. No two ways about it: Piper had definitely been favorably impressed. And she hadn't been the only one.

The story of how the new guy had dealt with the potentially nasty customer spread quickly through the P3 staff, right along with the rumor that Piper was considering offering him the manager's job. She'd been on the receiving end of secret thumbs-up signals from her staff throughout the rest of the night.

"Don't mention it," Gil said in the easy way he had. He took a quick swig of the bottle of mineral water Piper had provided. "Just doing what I hope will be my job."

"Oh, that's right. You came about the job," Piper said, with mock surprise. "And here I thought you'd just dropped by."

Gil laughed. Piper had to admit she liked the sound. Jennifer's assessment wasn't far off the money, she decided. Gil was tall and dark, with the sort of slightly rangy build that always reminded Piper of movie cowboys. His polish, however, would have been at home in a three-piece, hand-tailored business suit. Tall, dark, and smooth. It was a potent combination. And, she hoped, one that would prove positive for her club.

"Just so long as we're clear," Piper continued, "I appreciate the way you handled that situation, but there's no question I could have handled Mr. Grizzly on my own. Everyone who works for me pulls their own weight. They also all remember that I'm the boss. I don't micro-manage, but I do stay in charge. This is my place, and it means a lot to me."

"Understood," Gil said at once. "I know you took a chance, and I appreciate the fact that you let me prove myself." He took a sip of mineral water as if mulling something over. "Mr. Grizzly, huh?" he finally asked with a smile. "That's a good one. I have to admit, it fits him better than Norman."

"Please don't tell me his last name was Bates," Piper said.

"Nope," Gil said cheerfully. "Try Jones."

This time it was Piper who laughed. Then she sobered. "In your brief period of male bonding, I don't suppose you found out what Norman Jones's problem was."

Gil swigged more mineral water, taking his time, as if giving the question serious attention.

"Not to get all pop psychology," he finally answered, "but I'm thinking Norman Jones's problem is that he's Norman Jones. He struck me as the kind of guy who walks around thinking he's got an awful lot to prove. The trouble is, he hasn't figured out yet that proving something's just like charity."

"Don't tell me," Piper said. "You mean it begins at home."

Gil gave a quick, decisive nod.

Professional intuition, Piper thought. So far Gil had proved to be pretty intuitive himself. He'd finessed his way out of a difficult situation, winning over her staff in the process. Not only that, he'd responded precisely the way Piper had hoped when she'd made it clear she was in charge. She appreciated initiative, but she didn't want a loose cannon.

What, precisely, am I waiting for? Piper wondered.

"So, Gil," she said, "I know this really great club. Great owner, great staff. Trouble is, they're short a really great manager."

Gil set his bottle of water down on the bar with a click and leaned closer, his dark eyes dancing.

"Piper Halliwell," he said. "I really hope you're going to tell me more."

Chapter Five

"If that man says 'through the generosity of the remarkable Miss Lucile Marshall' one more time, I will not be held responsible for my actions," Lucile murmured under her breath. "Particularly as that's not what he means at all. Why can't English-speaking people learn to speak English?"

Halfway up the main staircase of Mural House, Phoebe bit back a smile. The speech making was over for the moment—at least the speech making on the main floor. Maxwell Harrington III's welcoming address had been every bit as flowery as Lucile had feared. Not to mention every bit as long.

Why was it that pompous and long-winded always seemed to go together, but pompous and brief never did? Phoebe wondered.

"You don't think you're remarkable?" she inquired.

Lucile gave a snort of laughter. "Of course I'm remarkable," she said simply, leading Phoebe to provide a laugh of her own. "And since I am, I hardly require someone else to point it out, particularly someone who's only doing it because he wants my money for future restoration projects."

"You mean rich guys can be brownnosers?" Phoebe commented. "Who knew?"

Lucile Marshall gave what Phoebe could only truly describe as a chortle. "Oh, I do like you, my dear," she said as she gave Phoebe's arm a squeeze. "I knew I would, from the first time we spoke on the phone. It's always so lovely when positive first impressions are confirmed, don't you think?"

Phoebe smiled down into Lucile Marshall's apple doll features and shrewd blue eyes.

"Absolutely," she said. "In fact, I couldn't agree more."

"Right this way, ladies and gentlemen," Maxwell Harrington III's voice boomed from the top of the stairs. "Right this way for the pièce de résistance."

It was all Phoebe could do not to laugh aloud as Lucile rolled her eyes.

Leave it to Phoebe to wind up front and center, Paige thought as, several clumps of well-dressed party-goers back, she trailed her sister up the stairs.

The two had gotten separated early in the

evening, shortly before Phoebe had first
attracted the attention of Lucile Marshall. True
to Piper's prediction, Paige had been attracting
plenty of attention of her own, but she'd been
more than happy to watch Phoebe operate in the
full glare of the spotlight. From the glimpses
she'd caught throughout the evening, Paige
could tell that Phoebe and Lucile had truly
bonded.

Though she was enjoying the fancy-dress
party, the truth was that Paige couldn't wait to
get home so she could regale her sisters with
some of the stories she'd overheard regarding
Phoebe's sudden attachment to Lucile Marshall.
Or maybe that should be the other way around.

One society matron, wearing a diamond
necklace that simultaneously managed to be the
largest, ugliest, and—or so Paige assumed—
most expensive piece of jewelry that she had
ever seen, actually claimed to know for a fact
that Phoebe was Lucile's out-of-wedlock love
child. The fact that Lucile was plainly old
enough to be Phoebe's grandmother hadn't
seemed to put a dent in the woman's enthusiasm
for the story she'd concocted. Not had it stopped
her pronouncements that Lucile's embarrass-
ment over Phoebe's existence was what had kept
the older woman out of sight for so very long.

Listening to the gossip swirling around the
room had definitely helped make up for the
fact that the most interesting guy present was

serving hors d'oeuvres, not eating them, Paige decided.

"As you are no doubt already aware," the voice of Maxwell Harrington III—whom Paige had privately dubbed Mr. Fuddy-Duddy III— continued to drone on, "though the main floors were public showrooms, the upper floors of Mural House were kept strictly private and served as studios and living quarters for the artists themselves. Our restoration efforts reflect this aspect of the previous life of Mural House, and at the same time they pave the way for its future."

This guy has got to be considering running for public office, Paige thought. He certainly had the boring speech thing down pat. Though, unexciting as the explanation was, Paige could see what Mr. Fuddy-Duddy meant right off.

The downstairs restoration allowed visitors to move freely throughout the rooms, but upstairs, the restorers had taken a more tradi- tional museum approach. See-through dividers enabled visitors to view individual artist stu- dios, but not actually enter them.

"Eventually, the rooms you see here will be made available for use by contemporary artists," Mr. Fuddy-Duddy went on. "Their creative process, and their work, will become a living exhibit during the hours Mural House is open to the public. The only studio that will not be used in this way is Isabella Marshall's own. One of the most private, as you will see, it was located at the very back of the house."

The forward momentum of the tour group came to a halt. A shift in the collection of bodies lining the corridor suddenly revealed Phoebe and Lucile's location, near the front of the crowd. In front of them, behind Mr. Fuddy-Duddy III, was an opulent red drape, completely screening Isabella Marshall's own studio.

As if sensing her sister's gaze, Phoebe turned her head and met Paige's eyes. Phoebe gestured with her head. Paige shook hers. Phoebe narrowed her eyes. Paige knew that look. It was the one that meant Phoebe would not be denied. Short of orbing, Paige was pretty sure she didn't stand much chance of reaching Phoebe and Lucile's location. Nevertheless, murmuring her excuses, she began to make her way through the crowd.

"As you also no doubt know," Mr. Fuddy-Duddy continued as Paige worked her way steadily forward, "shortly after William Lancaster's mysterious disappearance, Isabella Marshall stopped using her studio in Mural House. Though the room was always kept in readiness for her, she never painted in it again, nor would she permit anyone other than the housekeeper to go inside."

Slightly out of breath from her exertions, Paige reached Phoebe's side. "My sister, Paige Matthews," Phoebe whispered as Lucile turned to see who had joined them.

"Oh, so there are two of you," Lucile whispered back, her quiet tone nevertheless delighted. Before Paige was aware of what the other woman intended, Lucile had shifted position so that she stood between them, then linked arms with them both. The three now formed a connected unit. "How nice."

Out of the corner of her eye, Paige caught a glimpse of the woman in the enormous diamond necklace craning her neck in an effort to identify the newcomer. She could almost hear the woman's brain cells begin to overload.

Lucile Marshall looked soft, but Paige was surprised to feel how strong the older woman's grip was. She could feel the rapid beat of Lucile's pulse where the older woman's bare wrist pressed against her arm.

She's nervous, Paige realized.

"What this means, ladies and gentlemen, is that, with the exception of our restoration experts, no one has entered the room you are about to see for more than seventy years. No one would ever have seen *this*!"

With a dramatic flourish, Maxwell Harrington III reached up and pulled the red drape aside. The interior of Isabella Marshall's studio was revealed. In a sudden, spontaneous movement, the crowd surged forward. Paige felt Lucile Marshall take a false step, her grip on Paige's arm tightening painfully as she sought to regain her balance. Alarmed, Paige reached to steady her, making quick eye contact with Phoebe over the top of Lucile's head as she did so.

"No. Oh, please, God, no," Lucile moaned.

"Lucile, what is it?" Phoebe asked, her voice low but urgent. "Is something the matter? Don't you feel well?"

But Lucile didn't answer. Paige doubted Phoebe's words even registered. Instead, all the older woman's attention was focused forward, into the room that had once been her mother's studio.

"During the restoration efforts, a remarkable discovery was made," Mr. Fuddy-Duddy's voice soared over the swelling murmur of the crowd. "A full-length portrait of William Lancaster painted on the wall of Isabella Marshall's own studio. Even among Miss Marshall's other works, known for their lifelike qualities, this one stands out for its incredible attention to detail. It truly was her finest work."

I'll say, Paige thought. The man in the painting was so real, Paige had the feeling he'd do more than just the usual portrait clichés like breathe or follow her with his eyes. She half-expected him to walk right off the wall and join the party. And she could definitely see why William Lancaster had been a man Isabella Marshall—or any woman—would fall for. He had the good looks of a movie star.

His face was long and slightly severe. His eyes, a startling but unsmiling green, were offset by a full and sensuous mouth. Dark hair with an unruly tendency to curl swept down across his forehead. Like his face, William Lancaster's clothing seemed to contradict itself. The suit coat and pants were a severe and inky black; the shirt, a snowy white left open at the throat, as if he'd just removed his neckcloth.

Now there's a heartbreaker if ever I saw one, Paige thought. In her experience, men who gave out mixed messages were almost always trouble sooner or later. Usually it was both.

"As far as we know, this remarkable portrait never saw the light of day," Maxwell went on. "As soon as it was completed, Isabella Marshall obliterated her work, completely covering it up with the plain white paint that covers the rest of her studio walls. We can only speculate as to why. Unless, of course, there is someone here who can enlighten us."

He smiled in the general direction of Phoebe, Paige, and Lucile.

You sneaky devil! Paige thought.

She glanced down at Lucile to gauge her reaction and felt a jolt of pure adrenaline shoot straight down her spine. It was plain to Paige that Lucile Marshall hadn't paid one bit of attention to Maxwell Harrington III. All her attention was still focused on William Lancaster's portrait. The expression on Lucile's face contained so many different elements, it would have been impossible for Paige to name them all. But that didn't mean she didn't recognize the one at the very center, the one from which all the others flowed.

Lucile Marshall was absolutely terrified.

"The evil . . . the evil's been released," she moaned.

Then, as abruptly as she'd lost her composure, Lucile regained it. She stood up straight, shaking free of Paige and Phoebe, and looked Maxwell Harrington III straight in the eye.

"You fool. You pompous, arrogant idiot," she said. Then her eyes rolled back in her head and, gracefully as a silk handkerchief, Lucile Marshall folded in a dead faint to the floor.

The pain was back. Great, rolling waves of it. So strong it felt as if they would tear him apart. His head pounded with the effort to keep it clear. Lights as fierce and bright as torches danced before his eyes. Nausea, thick and choking, clogged his throat.

He reveled in it all.

The pain was glorious. The pain was beautiful, in an entirely different way from how it had been before. Then it had signaled his imprisonment. Now it was the harbinger of his release. And his revenge.

He could feel his body spasm. Feel a cry rise up from his chest, sharp and piercing as a knife. He wrapped his arms around his body, hugging the pain to him like a long-lost sweetheart.

He loved this pain. It was the proof that he had won.

Chapter Six

"She said 'evil.' I distinctly heard her say 'evil,' didn't you?" Phoebe asked later that night.

All three sisters were once more back in the living room at Halliwell Manor, following Phoebe and Paige's trip to the hospital with Lucile Marshall. With Lucile clinging tightly to her hand, Phoebe had ridden in the ambulance while Paige had piloted the family SUV, swinging by P3 to pick up Piper, the babysitter, and Wyatt. By the time they'd dropped Mandy off and returned to the hospital, Lucile had been admitted and Phoebe was ready to come home.

After an initial examination, the doctor had proclaimed that Lucile was fine. But because of her age, she was being kept overnight for observation. Though Phoebe had hated to leave the older woman, who looked fragile and pale against the hospital sheets, in the end she hadn't really had much choice. She wasn't a family member, and the hospital's guest policy didn't seem able to readily accommodate her. Not only that, as more than one nurse had assured her very firmly, visiting hours were over for the night.

If she hadn't privately agreed with the doctor's assessment that what Lucile needed most was rest, Phoebe might have been inclined to cause a scene and insist on remaining behind. As it was, she'd departed, promising Lucile she'd return first thing in the morning. Now, although it was late, the three sisters had decided on a quick family confab to fill Piper in on what had happened at the gala.

What little we actually know, Phoebe thought somewhat glumly as she shifted to tuck her sock-clad feet up under her on the couch.

While Piper put Wyatt to bed and changed out of her work clothes, Phoebe and Paige had retired to their own rooms to change from their party garments. Though they hadn't discussed it ahead of time, when they reassembled in the living room, the first thing Phoebe noticed was that all three sisters had chosen comfortable street clothes like sweats rather than the robes or pajamas that might have been the more obvious option, considering the time. It was almost as if each had instinctively recognized the need to be ready for action.

Now all we have to do is figure out what kind of action, Phoebe thought.

"I heard 'evil' too," Paige put in now. "The trouble is, we don't know what she meant by it. I mean, let's face it: People use the word 'evil' all the time and they almost never mean what we do."

"Fortunately," Piper said as she reached for one of the cups of herbal tea she'd prepared. All three sisters sipped in silence for a moment.

"She was looking right at that painting of William Lancaster when she said it," Phoebe continued finally as she returned her mug to the tray Piper had provided. "I don't know about you, but looking at that guy definitely creeped me out, even if he was drop-dead gorgeous."

"I'm with you there," Paige agreed. "But even so, I also have to agree with Mr. Fuddy-Duddy."

Piper choked on a swallow of tea. "With *whom*?" she managed after a moment.

"The guy who gave all the speeches," Paige explained.

"The really long speeches," Phoebe added with a smile.

"Somewhere in the middle of the second one, I think it was, I mentally christened him 'Mr. Fuddy-Duddy,'" Paige went on. "Anyway, right before he unveiled the studio and the painting, Mr. F-D made some remark about the portrait of William Lancaster being Isabella Marshall's finest work, in spite of the fact that she later painted over it. I have to say that I agree. I know it's a cliché, but—"

"He looked alive," Phoebe filled in. "Or as if he could be."

"Or wanted to be," Paige tagged on. She gave a quick, involuntary shudder. "There was just something about those eyes."

"Okay, wait. Let me see if I'm getting all this. Isabella Marshall painted William Lancaster's portrait, then painted over it?" Piper inquired.

"That's right," Phoebe said. "Specifically, she did this on her own studio wall. It was discovered and, 'uncovered,' I guess you could say, during the restoration efforts. Its unveiling was supposed to be this big, wonderful surprise. But when Lucile saw it, she completely freaked. Both Paige and I heard her say, 'The evil has been released.'"

"Right before she collapsed," Paige finished up.

"'The evil has been released,'" Piper echoed. "That doesn't sound good. You're saying you think the evil Lucile's talking about, which you haven't been able to ask her to explain, and the evil in San Francisco, which nobody can explain, are one and the same thing?"

"I'm not saying anything yet, because I don't know what I think yet," Phoebe answered honestly. She took another sip of tea. "Though I will say this much: I don't like it. There was just something about the way Lucile looked when she said the word 'evil.' As if she really, truly knew what it meant because she'd seen it for herself. The whole thing gives me this weird, itchy feeling at the back of my neck."

"It's that wool-blend sweater you insisted on

buying the other day," Paige said at once. "I warned you it might be scratchy."

Phoebe stuck out her tongue, but she had to admit Paige's remark had helped. Sometimes there was just nothing like a little sisterly silliness to clear the air. "Let's see what happens when we talk it through," Phoebe suggested. "Why would an artist as good as Isabella Marshall obliterate her finest work?"

"Maybe she just got tired of it," Paige replied promptly. "What if Isabella created the portrait during the first phase of her relationship with William Lancaster? You know, the giddy and in love part. Then, when William began to get all icky and possessive, she just plain decided she didn't want to look at him anymore. Particularly not glaring down at her in her own private space."

"Which would mean Lucile's reaction tonight *could* just be a reflection of her own bad memories, the shock of seeing William Lancaster again," Piper said thoughtfully. "She couldn't have been all that old when he disappeared, and children do have a tendency to view things in the adult world as larger than life-size. Once William started acting weird, Lucile probably found him pretty frightening."

"I can tell you one thing for sure," Phoebe said. "She still does. When Lucile Marshall saw William Lancaster's portrait tonight, she was absolutely terrified."

"Which pretty much brings us right back to where we started: why?" Piper said.

"That's a question only Lucile can answer," Phoebe acknowledged. "Something I'll try to convince her to do first thing tomorrow morning. In the meantime, I have to admit there's not much we can do."

"What about you, Piper?" Paige asked now, in a change of subject. "How was your night at the club?"

"Busy," Piper said succinctly. "Frankly, I think people are afraid to be home alone. But I actually have some good news to report. I hired a new manager. His name is Gil Townsend."

"What? When?" Phoebe asked as she sat up a little straighter on the couch. "Wait a minute. Say that again."

"I hired a new manager for the club," Piper repeated obligingly. "Just tonight. Yes, I admit it," she hurried on, as Paige pulled in a breath. "It does seem kind of sudden. But, actually, I've been on the lookout for quite a while. I just hadn't found the right candidate. Tonight he literally walked through the door."

"And you hired him, just like that?" Paige asked. "That doesn't sound like you, Piper."

"Not usually, no," Piper acknowledged. "I guess I must have been channeling the two of you. I totally went with my gut. Though only after Gil had finessed his way through a situation with a patron that could have gotten extremely ugly. By the time that was over, half my staff was in love with him. The other half thought I'd already hired him."

"So you did," Phoebe said.

"So I did," Piper confirmed.

Phoebe and Paige exchanged a look. "Okay, who are you and what have you done with my sister?" Phoebe demanded.

"The one who researched every baby diaper service in Northern California before she finally made up her mind?" Paige asked.

Phoebe nodded. "You got it."

"You guys," Piper said with a laugh. "It wasn't that bad. I did not."

"Piper, you still have an entire file drawer full of brochures," Phoebe protested.

"So?" Piper asked. "It was a big decision. Finding the right diaper service is very important."

"So is hiring a manager for your club." Phoebe held up her hands, palms up, as if attempting to balance the scales of justice. "An entire drawer full of diaper service brochures"—she jiggled her right hand up and down—"hiring your club manager on the spur of the moment."

Her left hand flew up. "You see my problem?"

"I do," Paige said.

Piper's head turned between the two as if she were watching a tennis match. A tiny frown snaked between her brows. "Let me see if I have this straight," she said. "You guys act on intuition and tell me it's a good thing, but when I do it, it's automatically bad. Am I getting this right?"

"Of course not," Phoebe said. "All we're saying—"

"I know what you're saying, Phoebes," Piper interrupted. "And, for the record, generally speaking, you're absolutely right. Doing things on the spur of the moment is not my style. In this specific circumstance, however, I think the two of you . . ."

Piper's gaze swung to include Paige.

". . . are going a little overboard. Gil Townsend didn't just walk in off the street. All right, okay, yes, he did. But he wasn't a total stranger. Danny Logan at Dockside sent him over. I didn't have time to do it tonight, but I definitely plan to follow up with Danny first thing tomorrow. In the meantime, however, I saw no reason to let a good thing get away, so I exercised my professional intuition and hired Gil Townsend."

"'Professional intuition,'" Paige repeated, as if mulling over the phrase. "It's kind of hard to argue with that one."

"Then don't," Piper said simply. She stood up. "Instead, let's all call it a night. Something tells me tomorrow's going to be a big day."

"I just hope Lucile feels like talking," Phoebe said as she followed Piper's example and rose to her feet. "I don't know about you guys, but there are a few too many mysteries around here to suit me."

"I hear that," Paige said. She switched off the light, plunging the house into darkness.

Chapter Seven

"Oh, my goodness!" Lucile exclaimed as Phoebe appeared at the door to her hospital room the following morning. "Those are very"—she paused, as if searching for the proper word—"bright."

Phoebe gave a quick laugh. "I was hoping you'd think so," she admitted. "Does this mean we can all come in?"

"I wish you would," Lucile replied.

Carefully, Phoebe maneuvered her way into the room. Above her head floated half a dozen shiny Mylar balloons with GET WELL SOON emblazoned on them. Each and every one was a different color. And each was shaped like a dinosaur.

"I intended to bring flowers," Phoebe confessed as she settled into the visitor's chair and secured the balloons to one arm. They bobbed gently above her head, giving off faint squeaking noises as they rubbed together. No sooner was she seated than Phoebe had to resist the impulse to squirm like a six-year-old.

What is it with hospital chairs, anyhow? she wondered.

Not one she'd ever encountered had ever been less than excruciatingly uncomfortable. Though she was sure there was some more official explanation, Phoebe's personal theory was that the chairs formed part of some secret government-funded science experiment designed to detect the presence of alien life. She'd certainly never encountered a human who could stand to sit in one. Fortunately, the distraction of the balloons helped.

"But when I saw these"—she gave their strings a quick tug and managed to shift her position slightly at the same time—"I couldn't help myself," she went on.

"I can certainly see why," Lucile said with a smile.

She's looking better this morning, Phoebe thought. Most of the color had returned to Lucile's cheeks, though to Phoebe's eyes, the older woman still looked tiny and frail, even in the single hospital bed.

"To tell you the truth, I don't think anyone's ever brought me balloons before."

"Definitely the right choice, then," Phoebe said. "Besides—" She gestured to a shelf near Lucile's bedside. It was completely filled with one of the most enormous flower arrangements she had ever seen. "There's no way I could hope to compete with that."

"I'll give you two guesses," Lucile said.

"Bet I only need one," Phoebe replied with a chuckle, pleased that her visit was starting out on such a relaxed, light note. "Mr. Fuddy-Duddy."

To her astonishment and delight, Lucile actually clapped her hands as she laughed. "Oh, that's perfect," she exclaimed, understanding the nickname at once. "How I wish I'd thought of it."

"Me too," Phoebe admitted. "Actually, it was my sister Paige. You met her last night."

At once, Lucile's expression sobered. "That's right, I did," she said. "Right before I . . . lost my composure. I do apologize, my dear. To both of you. You'll tell your sister, won't you?"

Phoebe made a split-second decision. "No," she said simply as she got to her feet and crossed to stand beside the bed. "I won't."

All the way to the hospital, Phoebe had mentally counseled herself to move slowly, but now that Lucile had given her the opening she'd hoped for, there seemed no reason not to meet the subject of what had caused Lucile's collapse head-on. Though Phoebe would be the first to acknowledge that she and Lucile didn't know each other well, or at least hadn't known each other for long, everything about her experience of Lucile last night was telling her that the older woman would appreciate the honest, direct approach.

"I don't mean to sound abrupt, but I just can't do that, Miss Marshall," she continued. "You don't have to apologize for having a normal human reaction. Not to Paige, or to me. I just wish you'd tell me what's going on."

"I thought you were going to call me Lucile," the older woman said, with just the faintest glimmer of a smile. She was silent for a moment, her fingers fussing with the bedsheets. "I don't suppose I could convince you it was nothing more than an unfortunately public and flamboyant senior moment?"

"No," Phoebe said. She smiled to take any possible sting out of her words. "But nice try." She sat down on the edge of the bed and stilled the other woman's fingers by taking them in hers, both pleased and alarmed when Lucile held on so tightly Phoebe wondered if she'd ever let go.

She really is *frightened*, Phoebe thought, and felt her determination to get to the bottom of the mystery ratchet up another notch.

"Lucile," she said softly. "Remember when you said I was your new best friend?"

"Of course I do," Lucile said, with a valiant attempt at a tart tone. "I'm old, not senile. Much as I do like you, my dear, I'm afraid I only did that because you were the only person I knew at the time. I know lots more people now. There's that nice young doctor who's been looking after me, for one . . ."

"It's too late, Lucile," Phoebe said again. She gave the other woman's fingers a quick shake, cutting off the flow of words. "You used the 'f' word: friend. You can't take it back now, so you might as well just give up. Something happened last night, didn't it? When you saw that picture of William Lancaster on the wall of your mother's studio. Something that made you both angry and frightened. I just wish you'd tell me what that something was."

"You don't know what you're asking," Lucile protested.

"Of course not," Phoebe replied simply. "How can I? But that doesn't mean I don't want to hear the answer. Let me do what friends do, Lucile. Let me help."

For a moment, Lucile simply stared up at Phoebe. Phoebe could almost hear the older woman's voice as she argued internally with herself. It seemed clear that Lucile wanted to confide in someone—maybe even that she needed to—but the reclusive habits she'd cultivated all her life were very strong.

"Let me ask you something first," Lucile finally said, her eyes on Phoebe's face. "Do you believe in evil, Phoebe Halliwell? I mean real evil, not the TV or movie kind. A force without pity or the instinct for mercy; that will satisfy its own desire no matter what the cost."

I knew it, Phoebe thought. In spite of the fact that she still didn't understand what was going on, in her heart she'd known Lucile's choice of words was more than just a coincidence. Lucile had used it because she knew what it meant. She'd had her own up close and personal view of what evil truly was.

"Yes, as a matter of fact, I do," she said, and felt Lucile's fingers finally relax as the older woman read the absolute certainty in Phoebe's eyes. "And, for the record, that's twice now you've used that word without explaining why. You know what they say—third time's the charm."

"There isn't any charm I know of to ward off this evil. Not anymore. That's the problem," Lucile Marshall replied.

Maybe there isn't, Phoebe thought. *But there are the Charmed Ones.* "Will you tell me, please?" she prompted.

For just a moment, Lucile closed her eyes. She removed her hands from Phoebe's grasp and pressed them against her face, as if wishing that she could hide.

"I'm an old woman," she said softly yet clearly through her fingers. "Old and alone. And you're right. I am afraid. Sometimes I think I've been afraid my whole life."

"I can't help with the first one," Phoebe said, and saw the fingers covering the older woman's face shift as if, beneath them, Lucile was beginning to smile. "But I think we're already on our way to handling the second one. You're not alone, Lucile. Not anymore. That just leaves us with what's behind door number three."

"So it does," Lucile said. She dropped her hands back down into her lap and opened her eyes. Phoebe looked into them, pleased to see that they were clear and calm.

"So it does," Lucile said once more. "Very well, my dear. I'll give you what you've asked for. I'm going to tell you a story, one that happened a very long time ago. I'm not certain telling it now will do any good, but I think . . ."

She paused and pulled in a very deep breath.

"I think that I would like to try to tell what happened. More than that, I think I must, while there's still time."

"You know about my mother and William Lancaster, of course," Lucile began.

Once again seated in the visitor's chair, made much more comfortable with the addition of a pillow stuffed behind her back, Phoebe gave a cautious nod. "I know what I read in the letters," she replied. "And what I've been told."

"Ah!" Lucile responded with the ghost of a smile. "That's what I like about you, Phoebe Halliwell. One of the things I first noticed when we spoke on the phone. Your mind."

"You and all the guys," Phoebe remarked.

Lucile's smile got a little stronger. Phoebe

could almost see the tension leave the woman's body. The combination of Lucile's own determination and Phoebe's relaxed stance was striking just the right chord to encourage Lucile to continue with her story.

"What you've read and what you've been told," Lucile repeated. "But I don't suppose it will surprise you to learn that there's more to my mother's story. What I'm about to reveal to you now is something that, to the best of my knowledge, only one other living being knows."

Only one other living being, Phoebe thought. Now *that* was an interesting turn of phrase for Lucile to choose.

"I'm listening," she said quietly. "Please, go on."

"You know about my mother and William," Lucile said again. "But there are two more people who make up the story. Without them, things might have ended very differently, though I still can't say if that would have been for the better, or for the worse."

"Two more people!" Phoebe exclaimed.

Lucile nodded. "Miranda Nance and Donovan Hawthorne."

"Donovan Hawthorne," Phoebe echoed as she sat up a little straighter in her chair. "I should know that name, shouldn't I? Wait a minute. I know. He was William's assistant."

"Very good, my dear," Lucile Marshall said. "Yes, Donovan was William's assistant, but he was also a great deal more. Devoted friend.

Faithful follower. The truth is that Donovan would have done anything for William. Anything at all. Died for him. Killed for him."

"And Miranda Nance?" Phoebe inquired.

"Miranda was a young artist, the last to become a member of the colony at Mural House," Lucile replied. "She and my mother took to each other at once. They became good friends right away."

She paused for a moment, as if casting her mind back, organizing her thoughts.

"I think, in the beginning," Lucile went on quietly, "that William and my mother were genuinely, unselfishly, in love. I could feel the strength of it, feel my mother's happiness, even as a child. The same way that I could feel her love for me. Does this make sense?"

Phoebe nodded. "Absolutely."

"This was in the early days of their relationship, of course. When they were most truly equals, working together to create Mural House. I don't think it occurred to either one of them that anything other than a brilliant future lay in store. But then something happened. Looking back, I think it started on the day of what should have been their greatest triumph: the day that Mural House opened its doors to the public for the very first time."

"I'll bet I can guess," Phoebe filled in while Lucile reached for a glass of water. "People saw the murals, but not the house."

"That's it," Lucile said. She set down her cup. "That's it, precisely. Intellectually, everyone knew that William's work was important, of course. But, just like last night, people didn't respond with their minds. They responded with their eyes and with their hearts.

"When you look at a beautiful painting, you don't stop to think about the frame that surrounds it, or the canvas it's been painted on. Not even the fact that the building was officially called the Lancaster Building made a difference. It was my mother's work that people noticed. Her work that they praised—and the other artists', too, of course. And with every accolade my mother received, William seemed to become more and more disillusioned, more and more bitter. By the end of that week, they'd had their first quarrel."

Lucile took a second sip of water. "It's funny, isn't it?" she asked rhetorically. "How much children see when adults don't know they're watching. Though my mother used to tease me, when I was little, about what big eyes and sharp ears I had. She used to call me her little owl. I think I understood there would be trouble, real trouble, between my mother and William long before Mama did herself. Though not even my child's imagination could have conjured up its form.

"Even then, I've always wondered if they might have managed to work things out eventually, if it hadn't been for Donovan Hawthorne. If I was a little owl, then Donovan was a cat, thin and sinuous. Always slinking out of sight around the nearest corner or door. Quite frankly, he gave me the creeps."

"I think I understand," Phoebe said, with a quick smile at Lucile's choice of words. "He was jealous of William's relationship with your mother."

"Yes," Lucile said simply. "And, to be honest, no. The trouble is, it was never quite as simple as that. As long as William's attachment to my mother brought him happiness, as long as it enhanced his career, then Donovan was content to leave things alone. But when my mother's work began to eclipse William's and this made him unhappy. . . ."

"I think I'm starting to get the picture," Phoebe said. "Did Donovan try to split them up?"

"On the contrary," Lucile corrected. "Though I'm sure he would have supported a break from my mother if that's what William had wanted. Unfortunately for all concerned, as it turned out, it wasn't. William wanted Isabella.

"Or, to be more precise, he wanted her shell, her face, her form. What he didn't want was her creative spirit. He didn't want her mind. He wanted no part of her that could give him any competition or take away from his own accomplishments. In that respect, I suppose you could say that William was exactly like my father."

Phoebe opened her mouth, then closed it again.

"Thank you, my dear," Lucile said with a faint smile. "Of course you want to ask. It's only natural, though I must say it's very good of you not to. Not everyone has been so kind. The answer to the question you've been thoughtful enough not to ask is really very simple. I went with my mother, I took her name, because my father didn't want me."

"Because you were a girl," Phoebe said at once.

Lucile nodded. "He wanted an heir and, to him, that meant a boy. It didn't matter that my mother's wealth—a great part of his attraction to her in the first place—was the direct result of Mama being *her* father's heir, his only child.

"Unfortunately for my father, my birth was difficult for Mama. The doctor advised against more children. But my father would never accept a girl as his heir. When she realized the depth of his feelings, how different from her own father he was, my mother did the only thing she thought she could: She divorced the man she had married, and we returned to San Francisco and my grandfather's house. She met William not long after."

"Which sort of brings us back to Donovan Hawthorne."

Lucile nodded, her expression grim. "It does. I don't know how Donovan and William first became friends, only that their bond extended back into childhood. Perhaps there was always something unhealthy about it, or perhaps that came later. That is something else I do not know.

"But I do know this: Donovan's devotion to William was absolute. For him, William's needs, his desires, came first. They had to be satisfied, no matter what the cost. It didn't matter that Donovan may have hated my mother—must have hated her, I've always thought. It didn't even matter that William came to hate her himself. What mattered was that, even through his bitterness, William's desire remained the same. And what William desired was to possess my mother utterly."

"But that's just not possible," Phoebe said, even as she felt a trail of icy fingers creep straight up her spine. "One person can't possess another. Not truly. Not completely. An individual always has free will, even though she or he doesn't always recognize that fact."

"You know that, and I know that," said Lucile. "William certainly must have known it. The letters show that, just as they begin to show the fact that his desire to possess my mother, to control her absolutely, began to slowly unhinge his mind.

"But what the letters never revealed was that Donovan promised William he would find a way to solve the problem. He swore that he would find the way to give William what he wanted: absolute dominion over my mother. Control of her mind and will. The power to substitute his thoughts, his desires, for my mother's own. The fact that my mother would thereby instantly cease to become the woman William desired never seemed to occur to either of them."

"Evil," Phoebe said.

Lucile nodded. "Yes, yes, it was. Since, as you've already pointed out, there was no natural way for William to achieve what he desired, Donovan had just one choice. He turned to *un*natural sources."

"Don't tell me he tried to make a pact with the devil," Phoebe exclaimed.

"Not quite," Lucile said. "But close enough. In his quest to give William Lancaster absolute control over my mother, Donovan Hawthorne turned to the dark arts."

Chapter Eight

"**The dark** arts," Lucile repeated softly into the silence that suddenly filled the hospital room. "Such an ominous, amorphous phrase, don't you find? It encompasses so much, yet explains so little."

Phoebe gave a snort of agreement. "You got that in one."

Unexpectedly, Lucile smiled. "I knew that I was right to confide in you," she said. "To wait so long. I've wondered, over the years, if it was simple cowardice that kept me from speaking out. But now I know the truth. I was just waiting for the right person to come along."

"I'm glad you feel you can trust me," Phoebe said honestly. "And I'm sorry we didn't meet sooner."

Lucile shook her head. "I'm not. I can't claim to be much of a believer in fate, in predestination, but I've never been quite happy believing the universe is entirely random, either. There's a reason why things unfold the way they do. Perhaps I've waited so long for the simple reason that I was supposed to. You are the one, the only one, I was meant to tell."

"There's more, isn't there?" Phoebe said.

"Oh, yes," Lucile Marshall answered. "I'm afraid there is. A great deal more."

"You said Donovan Hawthorne turned to the dark arts," Phoebe said, picking up the story where Lucile had left off. "Do you know what kind?"

"Not precisely," Lucile replied. "We could see its effects, once we knew what we were looking for, of course. But we never really had the time to discover its source. Without Miranda, we might never have known anything at all."

"You mean Miranda Nance," Phoebe prompted. "The young artist, the other person you said was important, in addition to Donovan Hawthorne."

Lucile nodded. "Miranda was the last artist to join the artists' community at Mural House. Though she was young, she'd been all over the world, studying the art traditions of native cultures. She'd been to places I'd never even heard of. There was a game we used to play. She'd tell me a place she'd been, and I would have to find it in the atlas my grandfather had given me one year for Christmas.

"But what Miranda never revealed until she felt she had to was that she'd used her travels for another kind of research as well. She studied the way the cultures she visited used magic, both to protect and to do harm."

"Wow," Phoebe commented as this sank in. "Talk about ahead of her time in more ways than one."

"My mother liked Miranda right away," Lucile continued, "in much the same way I took to you, I suppose. You remind me a little of her, in fact. She had the same direct gaze and direct aproach. Her studio was right beside my mother's, the only two at the back of the house. That's how Miranda came to overhear some of my mother's quarrels with William. She was the first to realize that something out of the ordinary was going on."

Lucile leaned back and closed her eyes. Whether it was to better help her remember, or because the telling of her mother's story was starting to take its toll, Phoebe couldn't tell. The impulse to tell Lucile to rest, that she would come back later, hovered on the tip of Phoebe's tongue. She swallowed it down.

I guess I just don't believe in an entirely random universe either, she thought.

Like Lucile, Phoebe believed that things happened the way they did for a reason, at least sometimes. That meant she needed to hear Lucile Marshall's story. Right here. Right now. No putting things off. Only by urging Lucile to continue could Phoebe discover whether the evil in the past and the present evil tormenting San Francisco were connected.

"Lucile?" she prompted, her voice gentle and low. "I know you must be tired. Would you like me to see if I can get you something to eat?"

Lucile opened her eyes. "You haven't been in a hospital in a while, have you?" she said drily.

"No," Phoebe admitted.

To her surprise and relief, Lucile actually gave a chuckle. "I thought not. If you had, you'd know better than to ask if I actually wanted hospital food. Now, let's see. Where was I?"

"Your mother and William's quarrels," Phoebe prompted.

"Yes," Lucile murmured. "That's right. They were terrible, those quarrels. I don't think I've ever heard such shouting, before or since. And they were always about the same thing: my mother's desire for a life, a career, of her own.

"Then, as suddenly as they'd begun, one day the arguments simply ceased. William begged my mother's forgiveness. He didn't want to lose her, he said. He admitted it would be difficult for him to accept some of the things that Mama wanted, but he promised to try. Frankly, I think Mama was so relieved and overjoyed, she never thought to question William's motives. Then, about a week after things settled down, the headaches started."

Lucile's own face creased, as if just the recollection of what her mother had endured still had the ability to cause pain.

"They were terrible in their intensity. It literally hurt my mother to open her eyes. Of course she tried to keep on working, but it was absolute agony. I used to hear her in the studio, sobbing as if her heart would break. Then, just like the quarrels, the headaches suddenly stopped."

"And where was William when all this was going on?" Phoebe asked.

Lucile snorted. "Right by my mother's side. Comforting her, doing his best to console her. I began to spend more and more time with Miranda, in her studio. We could hear William, when he came to call. Murmuring to my mother that perhaps the headaches had come on for a reason. Perhaps she was overexerting herself. If she would only rest, not work, for a while. I can still remember the way Miranda's face would turn white with anger when she heard him. But even that wasn't the worst.

"The worst thing was when my mother began to agree, and then to sound just like him."

Lucile shook her head, as if to dispel an ugly vision.

"It was horrible. I don't know if I can find the words to describe what those days were like. My mother's features stayed the same. I could still recognize her face. But when I gazed up into it, it was as if a stranger looked back at me through her eyes. A stranger speaking William's thoughts.

"She was thinking of giving up her studio, my mother said. It was time she settled down.

Set about the tasks she was born to do, the tasks all women were born for. Taking care of a husband, his children, their home. She'd failed at these things once, she said. She didn't want to make the same mistakes a second time. Wasting her time in selfish indulgences was only causing pain. Not just to her, but to everyone. She could see that now.

"Then, one day, Miranda found my mother standing in the center of the studio. She'd been working on a portrait, an important commission William had opposed. The canvas had been almost completely destroyed. Sliced to ribbons with a palette knife. My mother claimed she'd caused the destruction herself. She'd tried to stop, but had not been able to. She feared she was going out of her mind."

"She was," Phoebe remarked grimly. "More precisely, she was being driven out of it and replaced by someone else."

"That's exactly what it seemed like," Lucile concurred. "As if William had gotten inside my mother's head and was controlling her thoughts. My mother and William were supposed to attend a dinner that evening. Initially, Mama was too upset to go. But Miranda managed to calm her down. She should not mention the ruined canvas, Miranda said, but go with William as if nothing was wrong. Be charming and attentive, she counseled. Let William take the spotlight. Miranda would explain everything when my mother got home. My mother took Miranda's advice. As soon as she was gone, Miranda took me aside."

Lucile paused.

"I sometimes think that was the most remarkable conversation of my entire life. Miranda didn't treat me like a child. She treated me as if I were an equal, an ally. Someone who could understand anything that she might say. Someone to be respected and trusted.

"The irony, of course, is that what Miranda Nance told me on that night was something only a child could have believed so instantly and wholeheartedly. She said that William Lancaster was using magic to try to control my mother, which meant just one thing:

"We would have to use magic ourselves if we were going to stop him."

William,

What a cold, unfeeling way to begin a letter! As cold and unfeeling as you now accuse me of being, as if I did not long, once again, to call you my dear. But how can I do this, when both your heart and mind seem against me? How can I say that you are dear to me when you tell me so plainly, both by word and deed, that you do not value what I hold dear?

Oh, William! How have we come to this?

How has our love, so bright and shining, become so tarnished? Was it really made not of gold but of brass? Base metal that will not stand the test of time? That can never be molded into something lasting and beautiful, but only something easily scratched and cracked?

"Let me not to the marriage of true minds admit impediments." Our greatest poet, William Shakespeare, wrote that. You know this. You gave me the sonnet yourself, written out in your own hand. But now you tell me you wish there to be only one mind between us. No true love, no true marriage, but merely domination and subservience.

Faced with this, how can I say I love you? How can you love me and desire this? If you take away my mind, you take away my capacity to love as surely as if you cut out the heart within my breast.

Oh, William, I beg you. Come back to me, as you once were. Love all of me, as you once did. If you do this, there is nothing I will not do for you in return. Put me to this test. I will not fail you.

Isabella, written at Mural House, August 23, 1931.

Chapter Nine

As Piper needed to take care of some details related to P3, the three Ps themselves had assembled at the club following Phoebe's visit with Lucile at the hospital. Piper's new management hire, Gil Townsend, was expected shortly, but for the moment, the Charmed Ones had P3 all to themselves.

"So essentially what happened was that Isabella and Miranda turned the tables on William Lancaster. They beat him to the magic punch," Phoebe explained.

"How?" Piper asked.

"By pretending to give up the fight," Phoebe replied. "Actually, it was a pretty clever plan. Once she became convinced that Miranda was telling her the truth about William's not-quite-natural attempts at mind control, it was Isabella herself who figured out the way to get him to back off. Whenever they were together, Isabella gave William exactly what he wanted, a woman who was completely devoted. She even agreed to marry him and give up the studio, though not until after the wedding, of course.

"But at night, in secret, she was frantically working to complete the portrait of William that Paige and I saw last night on her studio wall. Once she stopped actively fighting William, he eased up on trying to control her. This gave Isabella and Miranda the time they needed to work their mojo."

"Which was what, exactly?" Paige inquired.

"I don't know the specific ritual," Phoebe acknowledged. "I'm thinking that's a Book of Shadows follow-up item. But the gist of what happened was this: As soon as the painting was complete, Miranda Nance cast a spell, binding William's essence to the portrait, trapping his will inside it. Then she and Isabella painted over it, sealing him up."

"So Miranda was a witch?" Piper asked.

"Lucile was a little fuzzy on that point," Phoebe said. "And, for reasons I'm sure I don't have to explain, I was a little reluctant to press her too hard about it. We should follow up on Miranda in the Book of Shadows too."

"Maybe you should start with her," Piper suggested. "Something in her background might provide a clue as to the spell she might have used."

"Good point," Phoebe said, nodding.

"Okay, I just have to say this," Paige put in. "Didn't William Lancaster ever suspect something funny was going on? I mean, one moment Isabella's fighting tooth and nail, telling him she wants a life on her terms; the next, she's completely agreeing to his. Wouldn't he find that a little odd?"

"Not if his ego was large enough, he wouldn't," Phoebe replied. "And my guess is that he had absolute faith in Donovan Hawthorne. We also have to remember that controlling Isabella, molding her to conform to his will, was exactly what William was trying to accomplish. He probably just thought his plan was working."

Piper gave a sudden shiver. "I wonder what he thought when he realized he'd been wrong."

"We'll probably never know," Phoebe said. "Though Lucile did say that, in spite of everything he'd done, she didn't think William had started out warped. He just got . . ." Her voice trailed off as she realized what she'd been about to say.

"Seduced by the dark side of the force?" Paige finished up.

"By the person he thought of as his best friend," Phoebe said, nodding. "Donovan Hawthorne."

"Who wasn't really his friend at all," Piper stated baldly.

"You can say that again," Paige declared. "After all, friends don't let friends practice the dark arts."

"What happened to him?" Piper asked.

"Good question," Phoebe said. "Not to mention a good candidate for Book of Shadows follow-up item number three. According to Lucile, Donovan Hawthorne disappeared the same night William—or to be more specific, William's body—did."

Paige and Piper exchanged glances. "Are you thinking what I'm thinking?" Paige asked.

"I am as long as it's *uh-oh*."

"There was a final step to the spell, the ritual," Phoebe continued. "One that Lucile said her mother refused to perform. Actually, that's the true source of Lucile's freak-out last night, combined with the painting being revealed in the first place, of course."

"I'll bet I can guess what the missing step was," Piper said grimly. "Destroying William's body. Or at the very least incapacitating it somehow."

"That's it, precisely." Phoebe nodded. "Miranda's spell trapped William's will but left his body behind, a mindless shell. But to truly neutralize William forever, Miranda and Isabella should also have, er, neutralized his body. Isabella Marshall couldn't do it. She simply could not bring herself to destroy the man she'd loved.

"According to Lucile, Isabella and Miranda actually had a pretty big falling-out over this. Before they could patch things up and find a way out of their dilemma, the place where William's body was being hidden was broken into and the body stolen. Three guesses as to who the thief was."

"Bet I need only one," Piper said. "Donovan Hawthorne."

"I do have to give Isabella full points for trying to do the right thing, though," Paige said. "Even if she did fall into the classic trap of good guys: the fear that, by behaving like the bad guys, you yourself become one. But by refusing to carry the ritual to its logical conclusion—"

"She left the job undone," Phoebe finished for her. "This means that—in theory, anyway—as long as William's body is alive, his will can reinhabit it, assuming it can escape the painting, of course. That's precisely what Lucile is afraid has happened: that the restoration of William's portrait has set his will free."

"The evil has been set free," Paige murmured softly, repeating Lucile's words. "No wonder she was so frightened."

"But the math just won't add up," Piper said suddenly. "Lucile herself is older than eighty. That would make William Lancaster more than a hundred years old. Even if we assume that Donovan Hawthorne did steal the body all those years ago, how likely is it that William could still be alive?"

"In the normal course of things, not very," Phoebe admitted. "But remember what Lucile said, that Donovan turned to the dark arts. There are rituals for prolonging life. Maybe Donovan used one of those. Or maybe it's even more simple than that. Maybe Miranda's spell, though obviously incredibly powerful, also had a really big loophole. What if, as long as William's will is alive, his body *can't* die?"

"Phoebe's conversation with Lucile has definitely cleared up some things, but we still have so many loose ends to follow up, I feel like I should be making a to-do list or something," Paige said.

"I think I've got the grocery list in my purse," Piper said. "You could add on to that."

Paige rolled her eyes. "I can see it now. Eggs. Milk. Bread. Rituals for mind control."

"You left out ice cream," Phoebe said.

"Nonfat frozen yogurt," corrected Piper.

"Okay, hold everything," Paige said. She gestured, forming a T with her crossed hands just like a football referee. "Time out. If we're going to get to the bottom of this, we need to focus, guys."

"I can't have ice cream?" Phoebe said.

"Piper obviously needs to stay at P3, so I'm thinking it's up to Phoebes and me to head back to the house and tackle the Book of Shadows," Paige said, working out the plan. She turned to Piper. "If there's anything we think you need to know right away, we'll call. If not, we'll pow-wow tonight at home, only this time we're having hot chocolate with those little tiny marshmallows."

"Only if you add them to the shopping list," Piper said.

"After mind control, but before rituals for prolonging life," Phoebe said, pointing to her purse. "We'll also pick up Wyatt and Mandy at the park on our way home," she added, before Piper could inquire. "You, in the meantime, will *not*—"

Before she could finish, the front door of P3 burst open and a lone figure dashed in.

"Piper, thank goodness you're not . . ." a voice cried.

Before Piper could think about raising her hands to put a hold on the situation, Phoebe swung around. In full-fledged battle mode she dashed across the room, then leaped, delivering a kick that knocked the newcomer to the ground. Then she planted a foot solidly in the middle of his chest.

"Piper," she said, her tone sugar-sweet as she glared down. "Will you please tell this guy I've never seen before who knows your name to identify himself? Otherwise, I'm afraid I'll just have to insert my foot into his rib cage."

"Wait. No. Stop!" Piper cried. Swiftly, she crossed the room, Paige trailing in her wake. To Phoebe's surprise, she knelt at the unknown guy's side. "Are you all right?" she inquired.

"I think so," he said, never taking his eyes off Phoebe. "What'd you do, hire a new bouncer?"

"These are my sisters," Piper said. "Phoebe is

the one with her foot in the middle of your chest. Paige is the more restrained one. This is my new manager, Gil Townsend. At least, I'm hoping he's still my new manager."

"Pleased to meet you," Gil said. "Any chance I could take a breath now?"

"Oh, geez," Phoebe said. She lifted up her foot and reached down a hand to help Gil up, assessing him quickly as she did so. She had to admit she could see why Gil Townsend had made such a good first impression on the not-all-that-impressionable Piper. In spite of the fact that Phoebe had managed to deck him, Gil definitely looked like he could handle himself, both with brains and with brawn.

"I'm really sorry for the overreacting thing," Phoebe said now. Gil pulled in one deep, deep breath as she went on. "The truth is, we're all a little on edge these days."

"Not to worry," Gil said as he flashed a somewhat cautious smile. "I can't remember the last time somebody managed to get the better of me, to tell you the truth." He stopped short, a pained expression spreading across his face. "Please tell me you're willing to believe that wasn't nearly as egotistical as it sounded."

"Absolutely," Phoebe said with a laugh, and caught Paige giving Piper a secret thumbs-up out of the corner of her eye. "What were you trying to tell Piper?"

"What?" Gil asked.

"You came in trying to say something," Phoebe explained. "Before you were so rudely interrupted."

"Oh, that," Gil exclaimed. "Actually, I was just trying to say how relieved I was to discover Piper wasn't alone. That's why I'm a little earlier than we'd agreed, in fact," he went on, turning his attention to Piper.

"Okay, wait, back up," Piper said. "What are you talking about?"

Instantly, Gil's pleasant face sobered. "You mean you don't know? It's all over the news. I heard it on the way over."

A thick silence settled over the club.

"There's been another one, hasn't there?" Piper asked quietly. "Another murder."

"That's right," Gil said, nodding. "As if that wasn't bad enough, it actually gets worse. The victim's name was Norman Jones."

It was taking too long.

He had tried his best not to let impatience rule him. Tried not to be ruled by emotions of any kind. Emotions were a liability, a weakness, a lesson he'd definitely learned the hard way. They were a luxury he had long ago ceased to be able to afford. Hadn't indulging in them in the first place nearly cost him everything?

But he was so close now to obtaining his goal! And the horrible irony of it was that the closer he came, the farther away his triumph seemed. The injustice of it would sweep over him in moments, thick and black and choking.

Those were the moments it was the most difficult to be ruled by reason. The most difficult to hold on to patience, to believe that the end to his torment was finally coming. Even more, it was actually in sight.

How long? he thought as he battled the pain, the weariness in the body that still refused to do his will. How long?

Chapter Ten

"Thank you for your cooperation, Piper," the man in the sport coat said. In spite of his street clothes, he had "police" written all over him. "You know the drill. If we have any further questions, we'll be in touch."

"You're more than welcome, Darryl," Piper replied, her eyes on his as she walked him to P3's front door. "I'm only sorry I couldn't be more help."

"I'm sure you will be, sooner or later," Detective Darryl Morris answered.

"Thank you for saying that," Piper said.

Finally! We're going to get somewhere, she thought.

Of course it could have been nothing more than blind luck that had brought Detective Darryl Morris to P3 that afternoon as part of the police investigation into the recent death of Piper's former customer Norman Jones. But somehow, Piper didn't think so. Detective Morris and the Charmed Ones knew one another far too well for either luck or coincidence to be involved, particularly in a situation as ugly as this one.

Darryl had been the Charmed Ones' informal contact on the police force for a number of years, and the relationship between them had managed to survive the deaths of both the individuals who had originally brought them together: Prue, Piper and Phoebe's older sister, and Prue's police detective fiancé, Andy Trudeau. Andy had died first, and Darryl and the sisters had mourned together, their grief forming an invisible yet insoluble bond.

Like Andy, Darryl had experienced some difficulty accepting the truth about the sisters at first. But when subsequent events had demonstrated all too graphically the very real dangers they faced, not only had he accepted, he'd cautiously agreed to help. Sometimes Darryl came to the sisters with cases that didn't make sense in the framework of ordinary police work, to discover whether or not some out-of-the-ordinary factor might be involved. The fact that they hadn't heard from him about the current murders had been both puzzling and somewhat alarming. Darryl did have strict rules of personal conduct, ones he never violated. But it just wasn't like him to hold out if he thought the Charmed Ones could help.

Though she was horrified to learn that Norman Jones was dead, Piper had actually been relieved to see Detective Darryl Morris come through P3's front door. Maybe he could fill in the details that would finally help the Charmed Ones get somewhere, provide the key that would help them fit together the pieces of the puzzle that, currently, seemed to float just out of reach.

"If there's anything specific you think I could help with, I hope you'll let me know," she said aloud, and watched as Darryl cast a quick glance around the club.

His team had already wrapped the interview with Gil Townsend and collected the names and phone numbers of other staff members who'd had contact with Norman Jones. They'd talk with some later, when they came on shift at the club. Others would be reached at home. Their tasks complete, Darryl's team was waiting for him outside. Gil was behind the bar, prepping for P3's opening. Standing near the front entrance, Darryl and Piper had as much privacy as they were going to get.

"Okay, Darryl," Piper said, her voice just above a whisper. "What's going on?"

"I'm sorry I haven't been in touch before now," Darryl said, careful to keep his own voice low. "And, for the record, my captain would have my head on a plate if he knew we were having this conversation. The internal security on these murders is the tightest I've ever seen it. We really want this guy."

"That makes all of us," Piper said. "Don't you think it's about time you told us what the police don't want anyone else to know? That has to be it, right? You're holding things back, hoping someone outside the force will accidentally reveal something they're not supposed to know."

"That's it in a nutshell." Darryl nodded. "Which makes it absolutely imperative that what I'm about to tell you goes no further than Phoebe and Paige."

"You have my word," Piper said solemnly.

"He doesn't just kill them," Darryl said simply. "He takes trophies."

At Darryl's words, Piper felt her throat constrict. "Well, that's disgusting. As if this whole thing wasn't disgusting enough already."

Darryl's serious expression grew even more grim. "You'll get no argument from me on that," he commented. "Here's the thing I think you ought to know, Piper. You know how this guy defies all the rules, killing across social and economic lines?"

Piper nodded.

"Well, he takes trophies in the same way. It's never the same thing, but it's always . . . major, I guess I'd have to call it. We're not talking rings or locks of hair. We're talking entire body parts. It looks to me like it could be ritualistic. That's one of the reasons things are so buttoned down.

The second the media gets wind of something like this, they're going to start screaming satanic cult killings and we'll have even more of a panic on our hands than we've already got."

"Ritualistic," Piper echoed. *Talk about coincidence*, she thought. *Or not.* Phoebe and Paige were home this very second, trying to discover which ritual had trapped William Lancaster more than eighty years ago. And now it looked as if a ritual killer was stalking the citizens of San Francisco. Maybe Phoebe's itchy neck intuition had been right after all and the two events were connected.

"Not to sound like a ghoul," she said, "but what's he taken so far? If it is ritualistic, then knowing what he, um, needs might help us figure out things like what ritual's involved. That could lead us to who, what, why."

"The first victim was missing eyes; the second, ears," Darryl replied at once. Without needing to refer to his notebook or any source materials, Piper noted silently. Plainly, the details of this particular case were ones not likely to be forgotten. "Then a woman with no tongue. Continuing the trend, the most recent victim's nose had been cut off."

"So he's going for the senses," Piper said. "Sight, hearing, smell. That just leaves one: the sense of touch."

Darryl nodded, his expression grim. "Norman Jones's hands had been hacked off. I know it fits the overall pattern, but it definitely seems to me as if this guy is escalating, Piper. He's got some bigger plan that we can't see. He's working up to something."

"And you want us to find out what it is," Piper filled in.

"You may be the only ones who can," Darryl answered honestly. "I'm not sure how much longer the department can keep details like this under wraps."

"Let's just hope we can figure it out before whoever's doing this claims another victim," Piper said. "I know you're taking a big risk here, Darryl. I appreciate it. Thanks for telling me what you know."

"I'd say it was my pleasure, but that wouldn't exactly be true," Darryl said.

Piper managed a smile. "Norman Jones was a big guy," she observed suddenly. "It would have taken a lot of strength to bring him down."

Unexpectedly, Darryl's expression changed. Piper watched as his eyes lit up. "I knew coming to you was the right thing to do," he exclaimed. "I don't know why we didn't see it before. That's what all the victims have in common: their physical strength."

"Men and women both?" Piper asked.

Darryl nodded slowly, as if working things out in his mind. "The first victim was a woman, a marathoner. The second was a longshoreman. Those guys are seriously tough. The victims don't necessarily exhibit the same kind of strength, but there's definitely a pattern. All the victims were physically strong."

Spontaneously, he swept Piper up into a hug.

"I've got to get back to headquarters," he said as he released her. "Pass this along. It may not be much, but it's something to consider. If nothing else, maybe we can arrange a press conference and tell the couch potatoes they're off the hook. Thanks, Piper."

"Thank *you*," Piper said. "If we get anywhere ourselves, we'll be in touch. Discreetly, of course."

Moving with his usual efficiency, Darryl left the club.

"Now that's what I call cooperating with the police," a voice remarked.

Piper jumped. She'd been so focused on the potential ramifications of her conversation with Darryl, she'd momentarily forgotten she wasn't alone.

"Actually, Detective Morris and I go way back," she said casually as she turned to face Gil Townsend. Gil was still standing far enough away that Piper felt certain he couldn't have overheard any part of her conversation with Darryl. But it was better not to further compli-cate things by trying to spin out some elaborate explanation when the simple truth would do, she thought.

"His former partner was engaged to my sister."

Gil's face lit up, as if intrigued. "Which one?" he asked. "Paige or Phoebe?"

"Neither," Piper answered shortly, hoping her brevity would help squelch Gil's curiosity. "Andy dated our oldest sister, Prue."

"When do I get to meet her?" Gil inquired.

"You don't," Piper said simply. "She died. So did Detective Morris's partner, as a matter of fact. Our losses could have given us an excuse to draw apart. Instead we've stayed close. That helps explain the little moment you saw. It was personal."

"And private," Gil filled in. "Oh, geez." Swiftly, he crossed to Piper, his expression chagrined and contrite. "I'm sorry, Piper. I've just behaved like a first-class insensitive jerk, haven't I?"

"Not altogether," Piper said. In spite of herself, she battled back a smile. There was just something about Gil that was tremendously appealing, even when he was in the wrong. Maybe it was his willingness to come right out and admit it, she thought. A rare thing, in her experience, particularly among guys.

"But you might want to consider curbing that insatiable curiosity," she suggested.

"I know, I know," Gil said, nodding. "My dad was always after me about that. I think he seriously considered having 'curiosity killed the cat' tattooed on my forehead."

"You and your father are close?" Piper replied, deciding to ask a couple of questions of her own.

Danny Logan, the restaurateur Gil had mentioned as a reference, hadn't been able to supply any background information. Actually, Piper hadn't been able to speak with him at all. He'd left for vacation early that morning. She didn't want to be sneaky, but a chance to get Gil to open up was too good to pass up. Companionably now, the two moved back onto the main floor of P3 and took a seat at one of the tables.

"We were," Gil said, nodding. "Dad's not alive anymore either."

"Any other family?" Piper asked.

Gil shook his head. "No. My mom left not long after I was born."

"That must have been tough," Piper observed. From personal experience, she knew how challenging it was for *two* parents to raise a child.

But Gil was already shaking his head emphatically, his expression as close to defensive as Piper had ever seen it. "We didn't need her," he pronounced. "Dad and I got along fine. He could have remarried if he'd wanted to. He never did. It was always just the two of us. I think it must be in the genes or something."

"In what way?" Piper inquired.

"His childhood was just the same way," Gil explained, his expression lightening. "Just my dad and his father. I think the men in my family just made bad choices when it came to women. None of them stuck around for very long."

"That sounds kind of sad," Piper commented.

Gil shrugged, seemingly at ease once more, though Piper thought she could still see lines of tension around his mouth and eyes. Piper was willing to bet Gil's father and grandfather had at least passed on mixed feelings about relationships with women, even if Gil hadn't made the same choices.

"Oh, I don't know," he said thoughtfully. "Kids are pretty resilient. They adapt to the status quo. I don't think my dad ever felt deprived by not having his mother around. I know I didn't. My dad was enough for me."

"It must have been hard on you when he died."

"It was, at first," Gil answered honestly. "But I adjusted. I got by. It's what he would have wanted me to do. What he raised me to do." Without warning, he smiled. "Now who's playing twenty questions? he asked.

Piper smiled back. "Guilty as charged." She stood up. "Whaddaya say we get back to work? After all, we do have a club to run."

"Excellent suggestion," Gil said. "I'll go finish up at the bar."

"Thanks!" Piper said. "I'll be with you in a sec."

Looks like I'll have a lot to share at the family powwow tonight, she thought.

My dear Isabella,

You see how I give you the cherished greeting you deny me? Yet you accuse me of selfishness, of preferring my own desires to your own. How shall I answer such a charge? My heart leaps to its own defense, asking countless questions of its own.

How can you love me, and not share my desires? How can you say you love me but deny me, all at the same time?

And you do deny me, Isabella. You know you do. And not you alone. Daily, praise is heaped upon your work, while mine goes ignored. But who created the walls you use as your canvas? Who helped you bring your dream of Mural House to life? It was I, and I alone.

But when I ask for something in return, when I ask you to set aside your own ambition to be my wife, you refuse. You must be free to work, you cry. As if marriage is nothing but a yoke and we, as mindless as beasts.

Yes, I wish I could control your mind! But only so that you might understand mine. You wonder if our love is not golden, but brass. But may not gold be melted down and re-formed? Re-form yourself to the image in my heart and you will never regret it. I will love and cherish you until the end of time.

I beg you, Isabella. Do not drive me to do

something we will both regret. On your head will be the consequences, not mine.

In spite of the pain you cause me, I remain,
Your loving William, San Francisco, 25 August 1931.

Chapter Eleven

"**Look, there** she is!" Paige exclaimed, her tone excited. "Miranda Nance. Man, I love it when this works."

"Me too," Phoebe agreed, though her tone was somewhat more cautious. "Now all we have to do is hope that finding her gets us where we want to go. Actually, getting us anywhere at this point would be nice."

"Start reading," Paige commanded. "Stop being such a killjoy. We're due for a break. I'm thinking this is it."

As they'd previously agreed upon with Piper, Phoebe and Paige had gone home after leaving P3, stopping only at the park to retrieve the babysitter and Wyatt. After settling Wyatt and Mandy in downstairs, Phoebe and Paige had proceeded to the attic to consult the Book of Shadows.

Though the Charmed Ones did many sorts of problem solving—individually and as a unit—the

Book of Shadows was still their bedrock. No matter how many times they turned to it for information, they always learned something knew.

Paige is right, Phoebe thought. Discovering that the Book of Shadows did, indeed, contain information on Miranda Nance definitely had to be considered a good sign. It had been Miranda who had originally proposed the solution to Isabella Marshall's dreadful situation. Not only that, she'd selected and cast the spell. This was a fact her biography was unlikely to include, but it might point the direction in which the sisters should search.

An anonymous ancestor had added Miranda's biography with a note that explained her presence in the book: The unnamed Warren witch had met Miranda at a gallery opening, befriended her, and learned of her relationship with Isabella and the subsequent disappearance of William Lancaster.

"She looks sort of like you," Paige observed as Phoebe began to scan the information on Miranda Nance.

"It's funny you should say that," Phoebe answered, her eyes still on Miranda's background information. "Lucile said I reminded her of Miranda. I think it's one of the reasons she decided to tell me the full story."

"So what have we got?" Paige inquired.

"The Book of Shadows confirms that Miranda was not herself a witch, though she did devote a significant portion of her life to documenting magic all around the globe. I guess you could call her a sort of gifted amateur. Her particular area of interest was spells that used an image of the human form as the medium through which the magic was employed."

"Makes sense, given that her other great passion was art," Paige commented.

Phoebe nodded. "This, in turn, led her to become an expert on spells of entrapment," she went on.

"Like painting someone's portrait, then imprisoning him inside it," Paige finished up. "I admit it's interesting, but it's not exactly new. It just confirms what we already know."

"We knew she'd used a spell of entrapment," Phoebe agreed. "But we didn't know she was an expert on it. That could be important."

Paige made a face. "Okay. Having a clueless attack here. I'm not sure that I see how."

"Well, one thing it might mean was that Miranda had a variety of spells from which she could have chosen," Phoebe answered thoughtfully. "That's part of what makes an expert an expert, right? Having a variety of tools and information at her disposal instead of only one.

"Not only that, Isabella Marshall and Miranda Nance were close. They hit it off right away. Without Isabella, Miranda might not have been able to join the Mural House colony. When she went to protect her friend, Miranda wouldn't turn to just any old entrapment spell."

"She'd use her strongest one," Paige agreed. "The one she considered the most likely to keep William Lancaster trapped forever."

"That's right," Phoebe nodded.

"So what we're looking for is the mother of all entrapment spells," Paige went on. "Preferably one that calls for the creation of a full-length image of the—what would you call him, the 'trapee'?"

"Wait a minute," Phoebe said, her eyes once more on the page that had Miranda Nance's own image. "Check this out. "According to the Book of Shadows, Miranda Nance left San Francisco in the early 1930s. That would be right after what happened at Mural House. She dropped out of sight for several years, but eventually relocated to Cairo."

"So the origins of the spell might be Egyptian," Paige surmised. "Well, that makes sense. Even in ancient times, the Egyptians had long-standing magic traditions."

Phoebe nodded. "To say nothing of pretty impressive works of art. Miranda could have relocated anywhere in the world. I'm guessing she chose Egypt because it had some special significance for her."

"So how do we find the spell she used?" Paige inquired.

"We ask nicely," Phoebe said. She pulled in a breath, then held her hands out, open palms facing downward, above the Book of Shadows. Paige stepped back to give her room, then stood on tiptoe to peer over her shoulder. "Firmly, but nicely."

Phoebe closed her eyes, concentrating her energy.

Ancient ancestors,
magic warriors,
aid me in my time of trial.
Reveal your secrets,
share your knowledge.
Show me Miranda Nance's spell!

"Please," Paige added in a whisper. "The truth is, we could really use the help."

No sooner had she finished speaking than, as if blown by a wind only it could feel, the pages of the Book of Shadows began to flutter wildly. Phoebe opened her eyes.

"Is it just me, or did it just get a lot hotter in here?" she asked in a low voice.

"No, I feel it too," Paige said as the wind began to lift both her hair and Phoebe's. "I'm thinking this is good, unless it means we're both getting hot flashes way ahead of time."

As suddenly as it had began, the movement of the Book of Shadows ceased. The air grew still and cool once more. Paige stepped to stand at Phoebe's side. Together, the two sisters stared down at the Book of Shadows. Two pages stood straight up. For the space it took both Phoebe and Paige to pull in one breath, absolutely nothing happened. Then, with an almost audible sigh, the pages parted and drifted down. Both Phoebe and Paige leaned closer.

"That definitely looks Egyptian to me," Paige said.

"Right," Phoebe agreed. "Okay, let's see what we've got."

"I may not like the math, but I'm afraid I have to say this," Piper commented later that night. "It looks like things are starting to add up."

"I'm with you," Paige said.

Phoebe nodded. "On both counts."

"You might as well say it and get it over with, Phoebes," Piper went on. "I figure you're entitled. Next time the back of your neck itches, both Paige and I will take it seriously, I swear."

Unable to help herself, Phoebe grinned.

"I told you so."

"The good news is that what Phoebe and I discovered today actually matches the first information we got from the Book of Shadows," Paige spoke up. "The murders are definitely not the work of a demon, though they are connected to the supernatural."

"Because both Donovan Hawthorne and Miranda Nance used magic," Phoebe completed the thought.

"I see that, and you're absolutely right," Piper said. "My brain still hurts, though."

"Have a cookie," Paige suggested. "That always helps me." She hefted a plate and held it out to Piper. "Not that these are anywhere near as good as yours, of course."

"Flattery will get you everywhere," Piper responded with a smile.

True to her word, Paige had supplied the refreshments for that evening's update session. Once more dressed in comfortable street clothes, each sister nursed a mug of steaming hot cocoa adorned with tiny white marshmallows. Not only that, to celebrate the fact that they finally seemed to be getting somewhere, Phoebe had suggested they go all out. The plate Paige held was stacked with cookies from the sisters' favorite bakery.

"So," Piper went on, gesturing with the cookie she'd selected, "let's do a quick run-through of what we think is going on. That way we'll all have the same, and preferably clearer, picture of what we're up against."

"And be more effective at finding the way to put a stop to it," Paige put in.

"Okay, tell me what you found out about the spell," Piper began. Before Phoebe could answer, Piper took a bite of cookie, then made a sound of sheer happiness. "White chocolate and macadamia nuts. Yum."

"Miranda Nance definitely wasn't taking any chances when she set about trapping William Lancaster inside that painting," Phoebe said while Piper polished off her cookie. "Though taking at least one prisoner is obviously what she had in mind. For life, if she'd had her way."

Paige nodded, then made her own cookie choice. "But that's where Isabella Marshall got cold feet and let her down."

"Lucile might not have been able to recall the

details of the spell itself," Phoebe continued, "but her recollection of how it was supposed to end was right on the money. In order to keep William imprisoned forever, Isabella Marshall should have made sure he had no place else to go. Simply put, that meant killing his body, which would have made it impossible for him to ever return to it, in the unlikely event he could break or undo Miranda's spell."

"You know," Paige said, her tone thoughtful, "for someone who wasn't a witch, Miranda Nance definitely knew her stuff. The spell she chose to neutralize William has incredibly ancient origins. It goes all the way back to the Egyptian myth of Isis and Osiris."

"Oh, wow," Piper said. "Talk about your major mojo."

"You're not kidding," Phoebe said. She began to tick points off on her fingers, as if keeping score. "First, you have the death of Osiris himself. He's killed by a jealous rival, then cut up into tiny pieces."

"Which," Paige put in, "get scattered pretty much all over. I think the words of the spell Miranda used are actually 'to the four winds.' But to return to the original myth, after Osiris's death is where his wife, Isis, comes in. She devotes her life to finding him—them . . . I mean, the pieces of him."

"And once Isis was successful," Phoebe went on, "she does what all the king's horses and all the king's men couldn't do for Humpty Dumpty. She put Osiris back together again."

"At which point Osiris does what any other guy who'd been murdered, then cut up and scattered to the four winds would do," Piper said. "He went after those who did him wrong and exacted his revenge. Miranda took an awfully big risk, didn't she? Using a spell based on a myth that sort of had a built-in case for revenge."

"I'm pretty sure she never expected it to come to that," Phoebe said. "And if Isabella had held her end up, it wouldn't have. But obviously, killing William and scattering his body to the four winds were more than she could take."

"Leaving open the possibility, however unlikely, that William's will might one day be freed from the painting and reunited with his body," Piper finished up. "A thing we're now reasonably certain has, in fact, happened."

"After Paige and I had confirmed the spell in the Book of Shadows, I checked with a couple people at the paper who were really in the know about the Mural House resoration efforts," Phoebe filled in. "The overall restoration has been going on for months, of course, but William's portrait was discovered only recently. About a month ago, in fact."

"That's about the same time the murders started," Paige said.

"My point exactly," Phoebe said, nodding. "I think there's really no doubt about it. We're dealing with William Lancaster. When the restoration efforts revealed the painting, they also released his mind. He's probably trying to regenerate his body right now."

"I'm afraid we can count on that," Piper said. "There's something else the two of you should know." Quickly, she outlined her conversation with Darryl Morris.

"The killer's taking body parts?" Paige exclaimed when Piper was finished. "Oh, ick. I did *not* want to know that."

"Not just any body parts," Piper answered. "Body parts with ritual significance. Even the police have noticed that. That's one of the reasons they've been keeping the actual details under wraps. The first four victims were missing, in order, eyes, ears, a tongue, and a nose. The most recent victim, the one who'd been a P3 customer, had his hands cut off."

"Touch," Phoebe said at once. All of a sudden, she sat straight up. "Omigod. I'll bet he's doing more than taking trophies. He's got to be . . ." Her voice trailed off.

"Consuming them," Piper said. "That occurred to me almost at once, though I kept it to myself. He's not saving the body parts he takes. He's ritually consuming them. That's the reason for the murders."

She paused to take a deep breath. "William Lancaster is trying to regenerate the body he was forced to leave behind more than eighty years ago."

Chapter Twelve

"I can't tell you how much I wish you hadn't said that," Paige said as she dropped her head down into her hands.

"You don't have to," Piper responded. "I'm sure we all feel exactly the same thing: a combination of horror and disgust."

"You can add fear to my list," Phoebe said. "We've got to find him and stop him. I know we just met Lucile a day or so ago. Actually, when you think of the situation in those terms, we've put this together pretty darned fast. But the murders have been going on for more than a month. We've got to find William and stop him. Permanently, this time."

"I couldn't agree more," Piper said. "The question is, how?"

"Wait, just wait a minute," Paige said. She shot up from the couch and began to prowl the living room in quick, tense strides. "Let's just talk about how for a moment. For example, how does a guy over one hundred years old take down all these people in the first place? Piper said she and Darryl figured out just today that the one thing all the victims had in common was that they were strong.

"That's why he, um, consumes them, right? To literally take in their attributes, have their strengths become his own. That's magic so old, it's positively primal. But how does he kill them in the first place?"

"Maybe *he* doesn't," Phoebe said. "Maybe somebody else does. William Lancaster's always had an accomplice. Remember Donovan Hawthorne."

"Don't tell me you think he's alive too!" Paige exclaimed.

"Paige, honey," Piper said soothingly as she patted the couch next to her. "Come and sit down. We're not going to get anywhere if we start freaking out."

"I'm not freaking out," Paige protested. With a sigh, she flopped down on the couch beside Piper. "But I admit I am feeling overwhelmed. I'm starting to think this whole thing would have been simpler if we *were* dealing with a demon. Those guys may not be nice, but, generally speaking you know where you stand. They're pretty straightforward."

"Actually," Phoebe said, "this may be too, if we really pare it down to the bare bones." All of a sudden her eyes widened. "I cannot believe I actually just said that. I'm so sorry. Calling Dr. Freud."

"You do have a good point, though," Piper said supportively. "This whole situation has had so many twists and turns, it's easy to forget it started out in basic human emotions."

"That's right. That's absolutely right," Phoebe said, nodding vigorously. "And I'm thinking it's focusing on those basic emotions that's going to help us solve it. As far as I can see, the ones involved here basically boil down to these three: love, jealousy, revenge."

"I think we have to include hate, as well," Piper said after a moment. "Donovan Hawthorne may have always hated Isabella Marshall. And I'd be willing to guess that, no matter what his feelings started out to be, William hates her too, by now. The fact that she's dead and he isn't probably hasn't changed that."

Paige nodded. "Being trapped inside a painting for more than seventy years just might do that to a guy."

"So we're dealing with the big three," Phoebe said. "Love. Jealousy. Revenge."

"There's never been any suggestion that Isabella Marshall died of anything other than natural causes, has there?" Piper inquired. In response to her question, both Phoebe and Paige shook their heads. "What happened to Miranda Nance?"

"As a matter of fact, I found out on the

Internet," Phoebe replied. "Miranda vanished while on an expedition to Alexandria. Her body was found several days later, nowhere near where it must have started out. In her studio in Cairo, in fact."

"Completely intact except for two things: Her tongue had been cut out, and her hands cut off," Paige said, picking up the narrative. "Not only that, every single piece of artwork in the studio, finished or in progress, had been smashed or ripped to shreds."

"No more creating images of the human form, and no more speaking spells," Piper murmured.

"I think that has to be it." Phoebe nodded. "And that's not all. Over the next few years, Miranda's artwork, which was in private collections all over the world, was also destroyed. It's almost as if somebody was trying to erase any record of her existence."

"And I'll bet we know just who that someone was," Paige said. "Donovan Hawthorne. But what I want to know is, why didn't Donovan go after Isabella Marshall, too? If you want revenge, why not go after the source?"

"But she wasn't the source," Phoebe countered. "At least, not the source of the spell. Besides, that's where love comes in again. Donovan Hawthorne was absolutely devoted to William Lancaster. What William wanted, William had to have. And, right up until he got himself trapped inside that painting, what William wanted was Isabella Marshall."

"There could be another aspect as well," Piper put in slowly. "We already know that William and Donovan were into mind games— literally, and no pun intended. Even though Miranda and Isabella ended up thousands of miles apart, my guess is that the art community at that time could still be considered a small one. Maybe Donovan decided it was more powerful to go after Miranda and let Isabella sweat it out."

"Spend the rest of her life looking over her shoulder," Phoebe filled in. "Which, in a sick sort of way, would mean he'd given William what he wanted after all: control over Isabella."

"But now," Piper said slowly, "both Miranda and Isabella are dead. Aside from William himself, there's only one other person still alive who knows anything about this."

"Lucile," Phoebe said. "You think she's in danger? Wait a minute. Dumb question. Of course we think that. It's the obvious conclusion to draw."

"But killing Lucile won't do any good," Paige protested. "She was just a child at the time."

"A child who knew about her mother and Miranda's plans and did nothing to stop them," Phoebe countered. "I think we have to figure on William's perceiving Lucile as an enemy."

"So what is he waiting for?" Paige asked. "Why not go after Lucile right away?"

"Now *that* is a very good question," Piper said. Both Phoebe and Paige fell silent at the sound of her voice.

"She's got a theory," Paige said in a loud whisper after a few moments. "I can hear her brain working."

Phoebe nodded. "Me too. I know."

Piper rolled her eyes. "All right, you two," she said. "This is the direction my noisy brain is going: This whole thing may be based in emotions, but it's been pretty darned organized so far. William's going about regenerating himself in a particular way. He's not just killing whoever happens to cross his path, then taking random body parts."

"Oh, for crying out loud!" Phoebe suddenly exclaimed. "It's practically as plain as the nose on my face. Why didn't I see it before?"

"You were focusing on other things," Piper said. "Such as whether it could be William at all. Now that we're pretty darned certain that it is, we need to change gears, focus on what we think is important to him. That's going to be our best way of tracking him down."

"Well, we know he wants revenge," Paige said.

"That's right," Piper said, nodding. "Not only that, it seems to me he's following a very specific game plan to get it."

"Which means two things," Phoebe concluded. "We need to find the regeneration spell he's planning to use. And we need to do whatever it takes to protect Lucile Marshall."

He was tired, and that surprised him.

All his life he'd been raised to be vigilant. Schooled in the need to give nothing away. To ignore pain, fatigue, even his own desire. He'd never violated that training, never even been tempted to.

And running through it all had been one central fact. He was a tool, and nothing more. His own needs, his own wants, were insignificant. The only thing that was important was the final goal.

Now, at long last, it was in sight. He should have been exhilarated. Instead he felt exhausted. Like a marathoner in the last mile of a grueling race, forcing the legs he could no longer feel to propel him forward.

Forward. That's it, he thought.

He had to keep looking ahead. Had to keep focused on the goal. Only when it had been successfully completed could he afford to rest. To sleep, and dream his own dreams instead of someone else's.

What will that be like? he wondered.

But his mind, usually so agile, so good at figuring the angles, all the avenues of possibility and escape, simply refused to stretch that far. He pushed himself to his feet impatiently. It did no good to dwell on what might be. "Might" was not a good word to count on.

Instead, stoically now, he began to move around the room, collecting what he would need for the night ahead. He had no time for his own dreams. Not now. Not yet. For now, he would do as he always had. The thing that he did best of all.

He would do what must be done.

Silently, he let himself out into the dark.

Chapter Thirteen

"**You're sure** this is absolutely necessary?" Lucile asked. "Really, I hate to impose."

"It's not an imposition, and yes, I am sure it's absolutely necessary," Phoebe answered, for what felt like the fiftieth time. "Not only that, it would be our pleasure to have you," she added with her best smile.

Convincing Lucile Marshall that her smartest course of action upon leaving the hospital was to make an extended visit to Halliwell Manor was turning out to be even more challenging than persuading Paige and Piper. But Phoebe simply couldn't think of any other way to keep Lucile safe. Of course she knew that having Lucile at Halliwell Manor would bring a new set of complications. That didn't mean it wasn't also the most effective way of keeping an eye on her. And of keeping her alive.

Eventually, of course, her sisters had been

won over. Protecting the innocent was their primary mission, after all. Not only that, if William Lancaster, or what Phoebe privately referred to as his henchman, did try to come after Lucile, having her at Halliwell Manor could literally help kill two birds with one stone. It would provide Lucile with maximum protection while drawing William and company out into the open, right into the arms and waiting powers of the Charmed Ones.

So far, however, Phoebe had yet to budge Lucile out the door to her hospital room.

"Look, Lucile," she said. She set the enormous flower arrangement, the one from Mr. Fuddy-Duddy, down on the floor. "I know we've only known each other a couple of days. Neither of us can claim to know the other all that well. But you leveled with me. You told me a story you'd never told anyone else. So I'm going to level with you now."

She drew a deep breath and looked Lucile in the eye. "I think you're in danger, and I *don't* think you need me to tell you why. Incredible as it may seem, you were absolutely right. The evil has been released. Sooner or later, you're going to be a target."

"All the more reason for me not to go home with you," Lucile said at once. "I'd be putting you and your sisters in danger. Didn't you say your older sister has a child?"

"My sisters and I can take care of ourselves,"

Phoebe said. "More important, we can take care of you. I can explain this if you insist, but I'll be honest and say I'd really rather not." She moved forward and placed a hand on Lucile's arm. "You trusted me once. I'm asking you to trust me again. Come stay with us, Lucile."

"I don't know. I just don't know," Lucile said. She gave a sigh and sat on the edge of the bed she'd so recently occupied. "All my life I've tried to stay quiet, out of sight. It wasn't my first choice, believe you me, but it was the only way I could think of to keep the evil that William Lancaster and Donovan Hawthorne started from spreading any further. Now you're saying it's all been for nothing, and you're asking me to risk you and your sisters into the bargain."

"It hasn't been for nothing," Phoebe countered. "You made a courageous decision, Lucile. One that I'm sure was enormously difficult and that came at great personal cost. What I'm saying is that now it's time to make a different one. Staying hidden to protect others just isn't going to cut it anymore. The evil's out, and I believe that, sooner or later, it's going to come for you. I know that isn't very comforting, but it is the truth."

"So you're saying I should make you and your sisters targets as well?"

"No," Phoebe said at once. "I suppose what I'm really saying is that you should acknowledge that you're the target, then let us protect you. If I didn't genuinely believe we could do that, I wouldn't ask it of you."

Lucile fell silent. "You want me to be the bait," she said finally.

"I might, if it comes to that," Phoebe acknowledged.

Lucile stood up. "Well, why didn't you just say so in the first place?" she asked. "Come on. Let's get going."

"You've already met Paige," Phoebe said a short time later. "This is my older sister, Piper, and her baby son, Wyatt."

"I'm delighted to meet you both," Lucile said. "Thank you for welcoming me into your home."

Following their departure from the hospital, Phoebe and Lucile had made a brief stop at the older woman's residence. There she'd collected a few belongings. Phoebe had been surprised at Lucile's choice of living quarters. If she'd stopped to think about it—and she had to admit she hadn't—she'd have assumed Lucile lived in some version of Mural House itself: a stately old Victorian mansion. Preferably one surrounded by a tall, ivy-clad brick wall.

Instead, Lucile had a condo on the top floor of one of San Francisco's most exclusive high-rises. The décor was modern and streamlined. Glossy photographs, both color and black-and-white, of pretty much anywhere in the world that Phoebe could think of, adorned the walls—those not already taken up with floor-to-ceiling bookcases. All were filled with books about travel, Phoebe noticed. Guidebooks. Picture books. Travel memoirs. There wasn't a work of fiction or a painting in sight.

The view was incredible, a full 360 degrees of the city. While Lucile put together a suitcase of necessities, Phoebe simply stood in the living room, slowly turning in a circle.

"I did that all the time when I first moved in," Lucile observed as she returned to the living room. She set a small travel bag down on the couch and moved to stand beside Phoebe. "At least once a day. I still do it sometimes. I may have made the decision to stay out of the world, but that doesn't mean I lost interest in it. On the contrary, I wanted to see as much of it as I possibly could."

"I'd say you did a pretty good job," Phoebe said, gesturing to the contents of the room.

Lucile was quiet for a moment, her eyes gazing out the window. "I did what I could, what I thought I must," she finally said. "If you'd known Mama, if you could have seen what knowing William Lancaster had done to her . . ."

Her voice trailed off. "Sometimes I've wondered if he didn't win, after all. She never forgot what had happened. It haunted her for the rest of her life. And it made me . . . afraid."

"That's only natural," Phoebe said.

"And equally natural to get over it, in time,"

Lucile answered frankly. "I never did. Every time I thought of going out into the world, of doing the things other people did, things like falling in love and raising a family, I'd see the look on my mother's face when she realized what loving William had meant.

"I know it's hardly fair to judge everyone by one person," Lucile went on, forestalling Phoebe's comment. "Particularly a man who turned out to be as disturbed as William Lancaster. But telling myself that didn't seem to make the fear any less. The truth is, I've taken the coward's way out all these years, Phoebe. And it's time I put a stop to it. That's a big part of the reason I'm coming with you today. If it costs me my life, at least I'll die a free woman."

"It's not going to come to that, Lucile," Phoebe said. "My sisters and I will do our best to see to that."

Now all I have to do is make good on my promise, she thought as she watched Piper and Lucile greet each other in the entryway to Halliwell manor.

"It's our pleasure to have you, Miss Marshall," Piper said.

"Lucile," Lucile corrected her at once. "Phoebe should have told you that."

"Lucile," Piper repeated with a smile. Wyatt gave a crow, his arms outstretched, then flopped forward into Lucile's surprised arms. "Looks like you've already made a conquest," Piper said.

"Goodness," Lucile exclaimed, plainly both startled and pleased to suddenly find her arms full of the wiggling little boy. "He's quite a handful, isn't he?" Wyatt wrapped his arms around her neck and nuzzled. "Not to mention quite a charmer."

"He takes after both his parents in that respect," Phoebe put in.

Wyatt extended his tongue and made a raspberry sound.

"I'm sorry I can't include my husband, Leo, in the introductions," Piper said. "He's away on business, out of town."

"I'll just have to look forward to meeting him, then," Lucile said politely.

A slightly awkward silence filled the hall.

"We weren't sure which room you'd prefer," Paige spoke up quickly. "So we thought we'd give you your choice. One at the front of the house, overlooking the street, or at the back, looking out into the backyard and what passes as our garden."

"Oh, the garden, I think," Lucile said immediately. "It's always a pleasure to watch things grow."

"Great. I'll just take your bag up, then," Paige said as she hefted it and started for the stairs. "Meanwhile, Phoebe and Piper can show you the rest of the house."

"If you're going to treat this as a social visit, it's never going to work, you know," Lucile remarked suddenly as Paige moved up and out of sight. "We'll spend all our time being so polite, we'll never be able to communicate when the chips are down."

At Lucile's forthright comment, Piper's lips quirked up. "Even if we do have ulterior motives for inviting you to stay, you're still our guest, Lucile," she said. "And it's our pleasure to treat you as one."

"Personally, I'd enjoy it while you can," Phoebe said, her tone conspiratorial as she scooped Wyatt out of Lucile's arms and returned him to Piper. "My guess is that the you-know-what is going to hit the fan soon enough."

"Anyone for a cup of tea?" Piper inquired.

"That sounds lovely, my dear," Lucile said, and beamed. With an impish glance in Phoebe's direction, she plucked Wyatt back out of Piper's grasp. Then, tucking her free arm through Piper's own, she steered her toward the kitchen as if she, not Piper, knew right where it was.

"Thank you so much."

Chapter Fourteen

"Are you all right, Piper?"

At the sound of Gil's voice literally in her ear, Piper jumped. Not that he'd had any choice but to stand close if he wanted to get her attention, she decided. Never a particularly quiet place when full, the noise level in P3 tonight had reached epic proportions. Yet another piece of the good news-bad news balancing act that had suddenly become the story of her life, and that of her sisters, Piper thought.

News of the most recent murder and recaps of the ones before it had been making the head-lines for several days now. Not surprisingly, the fact that the last place Norman Jones was seen alive had been P3 was drawing record numbers of people to the club. The good news was that it was good for business. A fact that definitely gave Piper the creeps but was, nevertheless, impossible to ignore.

The bad news was that that the entire situation had the whole staff on edge. Employees who, under normal circumstances, got along just fine were snapping at one another. The very air in the club seemed to have a weird energy, as if electrically charged. Piper half-expected to see sparks every time somebody in high-heeled shoes walked across the floor.

But worst of all, as far as she was concerned, was the fact that, following the burst of connections they'd made immediately following Norman Jones's death, the Charmed Ones' investigations had stalled. Though they'd gone back to the Book of Shadows, there was no entry that related to William Lancaster or to the regeneration spell he might be using. They were surprised to find some written by their ancestors, but they had to know specifically what Lancaster was planning in order to be able to counteract his plans.

Who knew I'd ever want to know there were so many different ways to reanimate tissue? Piper wondered.

"Piper?" the voice in her ear queried once more.

"I'm sorry, Gil," Piper said, raising her voice as she turned to face him. "I didn't mean to ignore you. I'm a little distracted, is all."

"Gee, I wonder why that could be?" he said, his own voice loud. As if to make up for how difficult it was to make conversation, he gave an expressive roll of his eyes.

In spite of herself, Piper smiled. The truth was that, though her sisters had had every right to be surprised by the swiftness of her action in hiring Gil in the first place, there hadn't been a single moment since then when Piper had doubted the wisdom of bringing him on. And even if there had been, it would have been entirely swept aside by the way he had handled himself in the current crisis.

Norman Jones's death, the inevitable questioning by the police, the record-breaking number of customers at the club—absolutely none of it had shaken Gil's good-natured composure. He'd even handled questions from the media with seeming ease, which spared Piper the need to do interviews herself—something she appreciated deeply.

Much as Piper hated to resort to clichés, the phrase "steady as a rock" kept coming to mind. Every time the combined weird energies of the different factions of the situation threatened to slide out of control, Gil had been there to calm things down.

"Have I asked you to remind me to give you a raise lately?" she asked as her eyes left his to roam the club floor.

"Only about every fifteen minutes for the last two days," Gil replied. "Don't worry, I'm keeping score."

"Ouch," Piper said. "Or maybe I mean, good. Things are so weird around here, I can't quite tell anymore."

"I hear that," Gil said, nodding. Like Piper's own eyes, Gil's swept P3, making sure everything was—and stayed—under control. "At least it means business is good. That's gotta count for something, right?"

"Right," Piper said. "The trouble is, it just feels so wrong."

"I know exactly what you mean," Gil agreed at once. "There's definitely some sort of weird gallows humor thing going on. The way I figure, it's just human nature. You can't fight it. So you might as well take what benefit you can, just roll with the punches."

"Interesting philosophy," Piper commented.

"But you don't approve," Gil said.

"I didn't say that," Piper protested. "I'm just not sure how far I could go with it, myself. Rolling with the punches has never worked all that well for me, though I'm certainly willing to admit there are times when it's appropriate."

"Such as now," Gil put in. Even through the noise level in the club, Piper thought she could hear both humor and resolve in his voice.

"Such as now," she acknowledged. "As in, for the moment. Overall, though . . ." She let her voice trail off with a shake of her head. "I guess that's just too passive an approach for me."

"Are you by any chance attempting to call me a girlie man?" Gil inquired.

Piper felt a quick burst of laughter swell inside her chest. "No, not at all," she answered with a smile. "I guess I just think that going with the flow only gets you so far. Sometimes you have to make a choice, pick a side, then stand up for what you think is right."

"As it happens, I agree with you completely," Gil replied. All of a sudden Piper could feel his gaze on her face, subjecting it to the same intense scrutiny he'd been giving the dynamics at P3. "I didn't necessarily have you figured for a fighter, Piper."

"Looks can be deceiving," Piper answered lightly as she felt the discussion sliding into dangerous waters. No matter how much she liked him and appreciated his efforts at the club, she wasn't about to discuss what she might fight—or why—with Gil Townsend.

"Something else we agree on," Gil observed.

"Bet I can make it three out of three," Piper answered promptly. "You see what's happening over at table twelve?"

Instantly Gil was all business as he turned to check out two sets of patrons beginning to argue over who had gotten to the briefly empty table first.

"I think the guy on the left is the winner," Piper put in. "Though I do feel like docking him points for wearing that appalling tie."

Gil gave a groan of mock dismay. "Which leaves me to explain that little fact of life to the loser, who looks like he outweighs me by a good fifty or sixty pounds. What is it about big guys and this club? I'm including a request for hazard pay in all those salary increases you keep promising."

"You got it," Piper said. "I'll go see if I can clear a space at the bar. Meantime, offer Mr. Big and his date a round of free drinks and your personal assurance of the next available table."

"Only if you quit telling me how to do my job."

Piper let herself laugh. It felt good, she decided. "No way," she protested. "I'm the boss. As such, I'm commanding you to get out there before they decide to solve the problem by sawing the table in half."

"Why didn't I think of that?" Gil asked.

Piper was still laughing as she made her way to the bar.

Chapter Fifteen

"**This is** going to work, right?" Paige inquired.

"Absolutely," Phoebe said.

From opposite sides of Paige's bed, the two sisters regarded each other somberly. Phoebe was the first to crack.

"There's no reason why it shouldn't work," she temporized.

"With the possible exception that not much else has, so far," Paige said glumly.

"Come on now," Phoebe protested. "We've got to think on the positive side. We've made some progress. Besides, we've been over our options about a million times. This is definitely worth a shot. I'm tired of sitting around waiting for the other shoe to drop, Paige. I want to *do* something."

"I hear that," Paige said, nodding. "And I have been practicing all sorts of new skills. There's no reason I can't take this on."

"There, you see?" Phoebe said. "I told you this was going to work."

"That's right. You did, didn't you?" Paige snorted.

The good news about the past few days was that no new murders had been committed. The bad news was that all three Charmed Ones felt like they were connected to a live bomb. *If* it would go off was hardly the issue. The issues were more like when, where, and the overall size of the blast zone. With their research into the regeneration spell temporarily stalled, and Piper so busy at P3, Phoebe and Paige had come up with a plan on their own.

"Lucile still otherwise engaged?" Paige asked now.

Phoebe nodded. "She and Wyatt are downstairs, doing *Baby Mozart*."

"We have *Baby Mozart*?"

"We do now," Phoebe said with a smile. "Lucile had it delivered, just this afternoon. Along with enough groceries to last about six weeks, and a fresh-flower arrangement for practically every single room in the house. I don't know how you and Piper feel, but personally I'm planning to beg her to never move out."

Any awkwardness that Lucile's stay at Halliwell Manor might have caused to any of the participants was completely over by the end of the first night. By the time the next morning had rolled around, all three of the sisters felt as if

Lucile had lived with them forever. Not only did she not pry, she went out of her way to help. As if sensing the area of greatest concern, Lucile had at once zeroed in on Wyatt. The two of them had bonded so completely, Piper had given Mandy, their teenage babysitter, a few days off.

Lucile might not have been as willing or able to take Wyatt to the park as Mandy was, but that didn't mean she intended for either of them to be bored. Before the end of her first full day at Halliwell Manor was out, Lucile had placed a number of telephone orders, resulting in a flood of special deliveries to the house, many of them for Wyatt. He now owned a complete set of the Wiggles and Thomas the Tank Engine DVDs. After he mastered *Baby Mozart*, Lucile was planning to move on to *Baby Einstein*.

But Wyatt hadn't been the only one to benefit from Lucile's largesse. There'd been treats for Phoebe and her sisters as well, mostly in the form of food supplies for the house. Here, as with Wyatt, Lucile had gone out of her way to be specific and thoughtful. She'd made certain to include everybody's favorite variety of coffee or tea. After discovering Paige's affection for hot chocolate with marshmallows, she'd gotten her some of each.

The hot chocolate was an extra-fancy mix imported from France. The marshmallows were handmade. The truth was, Lucile Marshall was spoiling them.

"I wonder if she'd let us adopt her," Paige said.

"Good idea," Phoebe replied.

"Do you think she'll mind it if we just ask her to take us at face value?" Paige went on. "Everything will be kind of hard to explain to our long-lost, newly found relative."

"Like why Wyatt seems like such a bright child?" Phoebe asked—although she thought her nephew would be the brightest child anywhere even without his enormous magical destiny.

"Come to think of it, she hasn't even met Leo yet," Paige realized. "Let's hope he doesn't just show up by orbing into the living room right in the middle of the Wiggles."

"It was a nice fantasy while it lasted," Phoebe said. "Now, back to work."

"Back to work," Paige agreed. "You've got the picture?"

"I've got the picture," Phoebe confirmed. "Let's open up the map."

Serious and intent now, the two sisters opened a San Francisco city map and spread it out on Paige's bed. After much discussion, the two had decided to perform a scrying spell.

Piper was actually the best scryer of the three, but her time was also the most limited, because of the hours she was required to be at the club. In addition, Phoebe had pushed her own leeway with scheduling at the paper about as far as it could go. She hadn't spent much time at her desk since the reception commemorating the reopening of Mural House. While inclined to cut her some slack at first, particularly because of her sudden closeness to Lucile, Phoebe's editor was starting to fuss.

Mural House was still big news. If anything, Lucile's unexpected collapse had made it even more so. And the fact that she'd fainted in front of the previously unknown portrait of William Lancaster had definitely added to the interest in William's and Isabella's letters, which were still providing the overall framework for Phoebe's column. A whole new batch of reader letters was piled up on her desk, awaiting her perusal. She could have had them delivered to the house so she could work from there, but to protect Lucile, they didn't want anyone coming to the Manor. Phoebe was going to have to report to work bright and early tomorrow morning.

Paige had been working a series of temp jobs, so she just told her agency that she needed a couple of weeks off. She hoped things would be resolved before then, but she wanted to make sure that she had time to weigh every situation so that she and her sisters would be ready for William Lancaster and could vanquish his spirit once and for all.

While she was thinking things through that morning, Paige had a brainstorm. It had come on so suddenly, then seemed so obvious once she'd thought of it, that she'd actually looked up, almost expecting to see the light bulb that had just switched on above her head.

She and her sisters had been waiting for William's next move, a thing that was pretty much the same as waiting for him to come to them. But waiting around was hardly the Charmed Ones' style. They preferred to take it to the bad guys whenever they could.

If William Lancaster wouldn't come to them, maybe they could go to him, preferably in time to stop another innocent victim from dying for William's twisted cause. Hence, the scrying spell. To aid in its effectiveness, Phoebe had returned to Mural House and taken a digital photo of William's full-length portrait. Then she'd gone to a nearby pharmacy and printed out two copies, both of which Paige planned to use in her spell. They wouldn't provide as strong a link as an actual item of William's might have, but they were all they had and therefore were definitely better than nothing.

If there was one thing Paige knew how to do, it was improvise.

"Ready?" Phoebe asked.

"Whenever you are," Paige replied, nodding.

In determining which spell to use, Paige had opted to stay as elemental as possible. Earth, air, fire, and water were the basics, and the basis, of many different kinds of spells. They were particularly important for spells that focused on the physical plane, such as locating and scrying.

But Paige had decided not to stop there. A scrying spell was more likely to produce a clear and accurate result if something associated with the individual being sought was involved. This was a luxury she didn't have. All she had were her copies of William's portrait. By invoking the four directions in addition to the four elements, Paige was hoping to balance out the odds.

She shifted position on the bed until she sat at its head, facing the map, legs tucked up under her as if she were sitting in front of a campfire. She braced her back against her headboard. To make sure everything stayed as stable as possible, she and Phoebe had commandeered Piper's large wooden bread board earlier that day. The map rested on this firm base, not quite covering its surface even when spread out.

Paige moved the first tools of the spell into position: four white tapers, snugly held in heavy glass holders. Their positions corresponded to the four directions marked on the map: north, south, east, and west.

A basin of clear water, the photographs of William's portrait, a thin gold chain, a handful of dirt from the gardens outside Mural House, and a box of matches stood in readiness on Paige's bedside table. She pulled in a deep breath, to center and steady herself, just as Phoebe switched off the overhead light, plunging the room into city-night darkness. The streetlights outside lit the room with a pale glow.

"Okay," Paige said. "Let's find this evil sucker."

With steady fingers, she picked up the box of matches, removed a single match, and struck it. In the dark room, its flare seemed incredibly bright. The sharp tang of sulfur stung Paige's nostrils. As soon as the flame steadied, Paige placed it against the wick of the first candle, beginning to murmur the words of the spell she'd chosen.

"North." The wick caught and held.

"South." Paige touched the match to the candle closest to her, at the base of the map.

"East. West."

Her movements careful and deliberate, Paige illuminated the candles one by one. In the still air of the room, the flames stood straight up, without flickering, bathing the map in a warm, golden light. Paige waved out the match, then repeated the four directions, continuing with the spell.

North, south, east, west,
Aid me now in this, my quest.
What I seek, reveal to me.
As I will, so mote it be.

No sooner had her words ceased than the candle flames flared upward.

"So far, so good," Phoebe murmured as she moved to stand beside Paige's nightstand.

Time for part two, Paige thought.

Never taking her eyes from the map, she reached toward the table at her bedside. Her fingers found the small pile of garden dirt Phoebe had gathered from the flowerbeds outside of Mural House. Paige scooped up a pinch, then cast it onto the surface of the map.

"Earth," Paige said.

She leaned forward and blew gently yet firmly, scattering the dirt to the edges of the map.

"Air."

Still without taking her eyes from the map, Paige reached out. Phoebe placed the bowl of water into Paige's outstretched hand.

"Water," Paige intoned.

With her free hand, she took the first of the copies of William's portrait as Phoebe held it out. Then, holding the bowl steady, Paige gently laid the photograph on the surface of the water. It floated, rocking ever so slightly from side to side. Paige held her breath. But the photograph stayed afloat, right where she wanted it. Slowly and carefully, using both hands now, Paige brought the bowl to rest on the portion of cutting board nearest her feet.

So far, so good, she thought. Now for the thing that would set it all in motion.

"Fire."

Once more she extended a hand. Into it, Phoebe placed the second photograph of William's portrait. Paige moved quickly now. Holding the snapshot in the middle of one side, she touched a different corner of the image to each of the candles, one by one. She followed the same order in which she'd illuminated them in the first place. North. South. East. West.

The photographic paper burned fast, the edges blackening and curling up. Just before the fire reached Paige's fingers, she dropped the fragment over the very center of the map. It was consumed even as it fell, creating a rain of fine black ash. Satisfied with her handiwork, Paige completed the spell.

> *Earth, air, water, fire,*
> *Call to me my one desire.*
> *Evil hides its face, yet I would see.*
> *Where it lies, reveal to me.*

No sooner had Paige finished speaking than several things happened, all at once. The surface of the bowl of water became choppy, as if swept by a sudden storm. The candle flames flickered wildly. Then, as swiftly as it had become agitated, the room calmed. The candles resumed their former, still positions. As Paige watched the bowl of water, William's picture slipped beneath the surface and came to rest, still faceup, on the bottom of the bowl.

"I think it's working," she whispered to Phoebe. Hardly daring to look away, Paige reached for the final item on the table at her bedside. A length of fine gold chain. Gold, for purity. She picked it up, then held it over the map, letting it dangle down. It hung down straight, as straight as the candle flames, which stood like sentinels around it on all four sides.

"Come on," Paige murmured, as if offering encouragement. "Show me. He's got to be here somewhere. Show me where his evil mug is hiding."

The chain began to sway, gently at first, then with more intensity. Without warning, the candle signifying East snuffed out. The chain leaped within Paige's fingers. She could feel it actually start to heat. The candle for South abruptly doused. Paige's hand jerked to the left, toward the West. The flame of that candle flared abruptly, then stayed high. North continued steady, like the North Star, a constant reference point.

"Ouch!" Paige suddenly cried. In the space of no more than a few seconds, the chain had gone from pleasantly warm to too hot to hold. Her hand spasmed, and she released it. It fell to the map in a perfect circle. As if imitating a snake, it wound round and round itself. Both the remaining candles went out at the exact same moment.

"Lights," Paige said urgently. "Phoebe, hit the lights."

Rather than go all the way back across the room for the switch to the ceiling light, Phoebe simply leaned over and switched on Paige's bedside lamp. Then she tilted up the shade so that the light fell directly on the map. The chain lay in a perfect circle. In its center, a tiny section of the map was still visible.

"We did it," Paige breathed, her voice hushed. "I can't believe it. It actually worked. We have a location." She leaned over, studying the map intently yet being careful not to disturb the chain. "It looks like someplace on—"

"Wait a minute," Phoebe suddenly said. She, too, was leaning over, studying the map more closely. "I know that location, and so do you."

Paige sat back. "Oh, no. Don't tell me," she said.

"I'm afraid so." Phoebe nodded, her own expression crestfallen. "That's the location of Mural House."

The power. There is nothing like it, *he thought.*

He could feel it, racing through his veins, stronger than the most potent drug, more intoxicating than the finest wine. Searing him from the inside out, cleansing him like fire. Almost, what he felt now made up for all that had come before it. Almost, he was ready for all that was to come. At long last, he would have his revenge. Just the thought of it made his hands want to tremble.

No! *he thought.* I will not give in to weakness, not even the weakness of my own desire.

Instead, he willed his hand to steadiness, strengthening his hold on the vessel he held. Slowly, carefully, his hand rock-steady, he raised the beaker filled with bright red liquid and held it up to the light.

So beautiful, *he thought,* this elixir of life, still warm. *And as he began, once more, to drink, to feel the power screaming through his veins, he felt his mind go blank, then fill with one overwhelming thought.*

It wasn't enough. It would never be enough.

He must have more, more, more.

Chapter Sixteen

"It was a great idea," Piper said early the next morning at breakfast. She popped an English muffin into the toaster, then poured herself a cup of coffee.

"It was a great idea, wasn't it?" Paige agreed somewhat glumly. "Right up until the moment that it didn't work." She plopped down at the kitchen table with a sigh. "Is it too early for a marshmallow?"

"I keep telling you, it did work," Phoebe said. She entered the kitchen dressed in the casual clothing she wore to work. The exception was her shoes. The fuzzy slippers she still had on instead made little scuffing noises as she crossed the floor. Phoebe got the largest mug she could find down from the cupboard, then poured the rest of the coffee into it.

"Got caffeine?" Piper teased gently as she retrieved her toasted muffin.

"Quiet," Phoebe instructed. She took a long, slow sip of coffee, closing her eyes in pleasure. Then, setting the cup down on the counter, she set about re-prepping the coffeemaker to make another pot. Finally, cradling her mug once more between her hands, she turned back to her sisters. "You were saying?"

"Actually, I think *you* were," Paige answered with a smile. Phoebe was always quite the sight before she'd gotten her requisite amount of morning caffeine.

"Oh, that's right. I was." Phoebe nodded. "I think your scrying spell worked just fine, Paige. It told us that William Lancaster—the strongest parts of him, anyway—is still at Mural House."

"Which could be considered both good news and bad news," Piper spoke up. "The good news is that he's still tied to the painting. The bad news—"

"Is that he's doing everything in his power to put an end to that situation," Paige supplied. "From an, as yet, still undiscovered location. How on earth are we supposed to stop this guy if we can't find him?"

"We have Lucile," Phoebe reminded her. "I think that counts on the plus side for us."

"I'm still not entirely comfortable with the general concept of Lucile as bait," Piper said.

"To tell you the truth, neither am I," Phoebe replied. "I know Lucile seems perfectly content playing with Wyatt—and don't get me wrong, I think she is. But she's also waiting for whatever's going to happen next, just like we are. Not only that, she knows she's likely to be a part of it. She used the word 'bait' herself."

"That was quite a speech for your first cup of coffee," Paige observed.

"I think I'm all worn out," Phoebe said.

"Your spell did do one other thing, Paige," Piper added thoughtfully. Picking up the plate on which she'd placed her English muffin, she moved to the table and sat across from her.

"It confirmed our earlier suspicions about the fact that, regardless of where he is, William has to have an accomplice. No way is he doing this stuff on his own. Not only is he not physically strong enough, psychically he's not yet in complete control of his own body."

She twisted in her chair to look at Phoebe, who was watching the coffee brew. "How's the research on Donovan Hawthorne going?"

"Slowly," Phoebe answered honestly. She turned to face her sisters. "In fact, I was kind of hoping I could hand it off to Paige. I have to go in to the paper this morning. From the dire e-mails I've been getting about the state of affairs on my desk, I think it's going take most of the morning just to dig it out. I won't have any time to spare before tonight, and I think we should keep going."

"No worries," Paige replied at once. "Just let me know how far you got before you head in to work."

"Of course," Phoebe promised. The sisters sipped their respective morning beverages in silence for a moment.

"I really hate to be the one to say this," Paige finally said. "But I figure we're all thinking it anyway, so someone's got to. Something's going to happen soon, you guys. And I mean something bad, the worst so far."

"I think we all know you're right," Piper answered quietly. "We can try to stop it—we have to try. But since we don't know when and where and to whom it will occur, it's going to be hard to identify the next Innocent."

"I hate the thought of losing another Innocent to this guy, but if we can't stop it, at least it will help us identify what the spell is," Phoebe said. "Which may finally provide a clue as to William's next move. That's it. I definitely need more coffee."

Stepping to the still-gurgling coffeemaker, she slid the carafe out from under the thin, dark stream trickling down from the unit's top and slid her cup onto the warmer in its place. Turning back, she caught the quick glance that passed between Paige and Piper.

"What?"

Whatever response either might have made was interrupted by the chime of the Halliwell Manor doorbell.

"What on earth?" Paige exclaimed.

"Maybe it's another of Lucile's deliveries," Phoebe said as she moved toward the kitchen door. Though the sisters usually left the door open, Phoebe had taken the time to close it behind her when she'd come down that morning. That way, conversation among the Charmed Ones would remain as private as possible.

So far, they'd managed a good balancing act of keeping an eye on Lucile without explaining how they'd be able to protect her if push came to shove. They were sure it would, eventually. It was just a question of how much would call for magic, and how much would be of the regular, everyday hands-on fighting variety.

"Though I do think before eight a.m. is overdoing the good service just a little," Phoebe added as she pulled open the kitchen door.

Through the now-open doorway, the sounds of the front door being opened, followed by a brief conversation, could plainly be heard. A moment later Lucile appeared, her expression startled but purposeful. Though the hour was early, she was already fully dressed with her usual neatness in slacks and a blouse.

"I'm sorry to disturb you," she said, her gaze taking in all three sisters. "But there's a young man at the front door. He insists on speaking to you at once. He says he's from the police, and that you know him. I did ask to see his badge, and he produced it. His name is Detective Darryl Morris." Lucile paused.

"Even with his identification, I didn't like to let someone who is a stranger to me into your

home, so I asked him to wait on the front step. I
made sure to lock the door behind me. I hope
that was all right. I wouldn't like to offend anyone."

Spontaneously, Phoebe swept Lucile into a
hug. "It was absolutely perfect," she replied. "For
the record, he's telling the truth. I'll go let him in.
Rescue my coffee cup, will you?" she called back
over her shoulder as she headed for the entry
hall. "And pour Darryl and Lucile a cup.
Something tells me we're all going to need it."

"It's bad, isn't it?" Phoebe asked several
moments later.

While Phoebe had admitted Darryl to the
house, Lucile had excused herself to go and
check on Wyatt. This left the Charmed Ones and
the detective alone in the kitchen.

"I'm afraid so," Darryl said, nodding. "I'm
sorry to be the bearer of bad news, particularly
at such an early hour. But I didn't want to waste
any time, and I think you'll agree the latest
development is definitely something you should
know about."

"Tell us, Darryl," Piper said. She placed a cup
of coffee and a toasted English muffin in front of
him. She'd relinquished her own place at the
table to Darryl as soon as he'd arrived. As she
watched her older sister move swiftly and effi-
ciently around the kitchen, Phoebe felt an unexpected warm glow.

Piper's attentions were more than just ges-
tures of hospitality, though she was always con-
siderate and welcoming of others. When the
going got tough, Piper always found the way to
use simple actions to nurture, to keep the positive alive. It was one of the things Phoebe loved
and appreciated most about her.

Before Darryl could reply, Lucile reappeared
in the kitchen doorway. "He's fine," she said
simply, in response to the question in Piper's
eyes. "I left him set up with *Baby Mozart.* He's
actually humming along. I wouldn't be surprised if he comes up with a symphony of his
own by the end of the week."

"Wyatt is full of surprises," Piper said with a
smile.

An uncertain silence filled the kitchen. Darryl
took a sip of coffee. Lucile hesitated by the
kitchen door. The expression on her face was
determined and slightly mutinous, as if she was
expecting a fight.

"You two were never officially introduced,
were you?" Phoebe said suddenly. "Lucile, this
is Detective Darryl Morris. He's an old friend of
the family, in addition to being one of San
Francisco's finest."

"I'm not that old," Darryl protested with a
smile.

"Darryl, this is Lucile Marshall."

"I'm pleased to meet you, ma'am," Darryl
said politely.

"And I you, Detective," Lucile responded.

A second silence fell.

"You've come about these terrible murders, haven't you?" Lucile asked.

"Yes. Yes, I have," Darryl answered honestly. "With all respect, that's why I think it might be best—" he began.

"It's all right, Darryl. You can speak freely in front of Lucile," Phoebe suddenly interrupted.

Darryl set his coffee cup down with a *clink*, his expression plainly surprised.

"We think Lucile may be a part of the larger scheme of things through her mother, Isabella Marshall," Piper filled in quietly. Her eyes met Phoebe's and held. In them, Phoebe read both approval and a warning. She gave a small nod to show she understood.

"You think the murders are related to Mural House?" Darryl asked, his tone surprised.

"We do, actually." Paige nodded. "But it's a very long story we probably don't have time for now."

"Oka-ay," Darryl said, drawing the word out. "I guess I can buy that." Unexpectedly, he grinned. "It's not as if I haven't heard that line before, after all."

"Lucile and I met through my work at the paper," Phoebe filled in as she pulled out a chair for Lucile and gestured for her to sit down. "She knows we're looking into the situation, but we haven't really gotten into explaining our actual methods. But because we thought she might be connected, we also thought she'd be better off staying with us."

"Okay," Darryl said again, the syllables brisk this time. "I see."

Phoebe felt a quick spurt of relief. Darryl's response showed he'd understood at once the unspoken part of Phoebe's message. Lucile was aware that Phoebe and her sisters were interested in the supernatural, but she didn't know that they were witches, that they actually had powers of their own. As he provided the information he'd come to relay, Darryl would now take care not to tip her off.

In the long run, Phoebe felt absolutely certain that Lucile would be able to handle the news. But in the short run, the fewer people who knew the truth about Phoebe and her sisters, the better. That was a standing rule of the Charmed Ones. Besides, unless Phoebe missed her guess, what Darryl was about to share would not be pleasant. There were only so many shocks a person could take in one morning.

"We're ready whenever you are, Detective," she said. As if in solidarity, she moved to stand behind Lucile, resting one hand on the back of her chair. Piper moved to sit beside Paige, across the table from Darryl. Detective Darryl Morris was now the focus of four pairs of concerned yet steady eyes.

"I probably don't have to tell you the first part of why I'm here," he said simply. "There's been another murder. It was discovered early this morning. We believe it took place sometime between two and four a.m."

"So you were able to be on the scene almost at once," Paige spoke up.

Darryl nodded. "That's right. This isn't always the case, as you know. There's no nice or easy way to say this," he said, "but as it turned out, there was a specific reason we were alerted so quickly."

Darryl paused. His eyes met Phoebe's briefly, as if seeking confirmation that Lucile would really be able to handle whatever came next. Phoebe gave a small but reassuring nod.

"A neighbor called it in," Darryl said simply. "He was coming home late from a night on the town. There's been a lot of that going around lately," he commented, with a glance at Piper.

"As we both know," she said, nodding.

"So our neighbor gets off the elevator and heads down the hall to his apartment," Darryl went on. "It's an okay building—not fancy, but not a dive. The hallway lighting is dim but functional, and definitely bright enough for him to notice something strange across the hall."

"What sort of something strange?" Phoebe asked.

"A very large stain on the hall carpet that

seemed to be coming from underneath his neighbor's door."

At Darryl's words, Phoebe felt a tingle shoot straight down her spine. Gooseflesh stood up on her arms. But it was Piper who actually spoke first.

"Blood," she said.

"A lot of blood," Darryl confirmed at once. "More than any one person could lose and still be alive, a thing we confirmed moments after entering the apartment. But even then—"

"It wasn't enough."

This time Phoebe was the one to interrupt. She'd known where Darryl was going the moment he'd mentioned the stain.

"My guess is, your experts are already telling you that they think the amount of blood actually found at the scene and the amount that *should* be there don't add up."

"That's right," Darryl nodded.

Lucile made a soft sound of dismay. Phoebe squeezed her shoulder reassuringly.

"How did the victim die?" Paige inquired. "Other than loss of blood, I mean."

This time, Darryl looked directly at Lucile. "Are you *sure* you want to stay, ma'am?" he inquired.

"Thank you for asking, Detective. But, yes, I will stay," Lucile replied in a quiet, firm voice. "I do appreciate your concern. You're very thoughtful. Now please tell us how this poor person died."

"Her throat was cut," Darryl answered, his words simple and stark. "Literally from ear to ear. Whoever did this almost took her head off."

"What a horrible way to die," Lucile said. "God rest her soul."

"The victim was a woman?" Piper asked for confirmation.

"And not just any woman," Darryl responded with a nod. "Her name was Gloria Mashuto, and she was the Northern California women's middle-weight division boxing champion."

"Which fits the pattern," Piper completed the thought. "She was strong." She stood up. "I'm going to get the list of regeneration spells we were considering," she said. "Be right back."

She left the room at a brisk walk.

"After your first conversation with Piper, we did some research," Paige explained while Piper was gone. "We came to the conclusion that you were right to think the murders might have some ritual significance."

"Specifically," Phoebe picked up the thread, "we believe that the ultimate reason for these murders may be to provide fuel, I guess you could say, for a regeneration spell."

Lucile made another sound of dismay, as if realizing at once the significance of what Phoebe's words implied.

"The trouble is," Phoebe continued, "there are an awful lot of regeneration spells. They all have important variations. We haven't been able to narrow the field down to one. The best we could do were our top five choices. Horrible as it is, this latest murder may provide us with the clue we need to settle the matter of the spell once and for all."

"Which will bring us one step closer to the killer," Paige finished up. "In theory, anyhow."

"A regeneration spell," Darryl echoed. "But wouldn't that mean—"

"Okay," Piper said, her voice slicing through Darryl's as she hurried back into the room. "I think we've got it." She resumed her position beside Paige, slapping a simple, wire-bound notebook onto the center of the kitchen table as she did so. "Take a look at number four. They told you about the list?" she asked Darryl as he leaned closer.

"Yep," he answered with a nod.

Phoebe grabbed a chair and slid it between Lucile and Darryl, giving the older woman's arm a reassuring squeeze as she did so. Everyone at the table regarded Piper's list in silence for a moment. Faintly, in the background, could be heard the sounds of Wyatt's *Baby Mozart.*

"Well, this is definitely creepy," Darryl finally said. "In more ways than one. For example, how come they all look so much like recipes?"

"My fault," Piper said at once. "I was trying to keep things short and simple. What body parts were needed, in what order, what would be the short-term results, if any, and, finally, the ultimate goal. The recipe format just seemed to fit."

"I think you're right, Piper," Paige spoke up. "I mean about it being number four. That's the only one where all the, er, ingredients add up. Not only that, they're in the right order."

"And check that out," Phoebe said, pointing. "Look at the ultimate goal: eternal life *and* eternal youth. I don't know about the rest of you, but I'm thinking that definitely sounds like our boy. He'll get back all the things that he feels were stolen from him, and then some."

"But before that can happen," Lucile Marshall spoke up suddenly, "he needs one item more. The thing that will truly give him the ultimate revenge: his enemy's heart. I think we all know what that means."

"Neither your mother nor Miranda is alive any longer," Phoebe confirmed quietly. "Which, I'm afraid, pretty much leaves both William and all of us with the obvious choice."

"It has to be my heart," Lucile said simply. "I'm the only one of the original trio left alive. For William to truly triumph, to have both his revenge and eternal life, he's going to have to"— she leaned over Piper's notebook as if to refresh her memory—"cut my heart out and eat it while it's still beating."

Solemnly, her eyes moved around the table. "I

don't know about the rest of you, but all I can say is, over my dead body."

"I'd like to add something to that, if I may," Darryl said.

"By all means," Lucile replied.

"Gross."

Chapter Seventeen

"I still don't like leaving you," Phoebe said. "It just doesn't seem right."

"Stop fussing, Phoebe," Lucile said calmly. Standing in the living room at Halliwell Manor, she held out the light jacket Phoebe had selected to wear to work and gave it a little shake, as if to encourage her to put it on.

Darryl had departed about half an hour before. Not many of the specifics he'd discussed with the Charmed Ones could be shared at police headquarters, though he had taken with him a copy of the regeneration spell. Already somewhat notorious in the department for the unusual information he provided on occasion, Darryl could always claim the research on the spell had been his own. If nothing else, it would provide the police profilers with confirmation of their ritual-killing theory.

"It was bound to happen sooner or later, and

it's not as if you're leaving me on my own," Lucile went on.

"That's right," Paige said. "She'll still have us. Piper will be here until she has to leave for the club. And Wyatt and I will be here all day, won't we, big guy?" From across the room, she gave him a grin. "He'll be doing *Baby Einstein,* and I'll be researching Donovan Hawthorne. Between the two of us, we'll have this case cracked wide open by the time you get home."

"I know, I know all that," Phoebe said. "Okay, I didn't know today was the day Wyatt moved on to *Baby Einstein.* But I still feel responsible for you, Lucile. After all, I'm the one who brought you home."

"You make me sound like a lost kitten," Lucile remarked, her tone tart. "I am a bit more capable than that, you know."

"Of course I do," Phoebe said at once. "It's just . . . I promised we'd keep you safe. I wanted to be here in person to follow through myself."

"And so you have," Lucile said as she nudged Phoebe's second arm into the sleeve of the coat. "And I appreciate it more than you can know. There's been no one to look after me in a very long time. The fact that you were all willing to do so now . . ." Her voice trailed off.

"*Are* willing," Piper spoke up.

"Thank you, my dear," Lucile said. "Thank you very much. And I'd like to stay safe, believe you me. Nevertheless, I can't help but wonder . . .

keeping me safe isn't really getting us anywhere, is it? And the fact that I am the only one who might be able to draw William out of hiding does seem rather obvious. The possibility that I might need to serve as bait has been there all along. Maybe it's time to do something about it."

"Such as what?" Phoebe inquired.

Lucile threw up her hands and plunked down on the couch. "That's the problem, of course. I simply don't know. I want to be useful, and I definitely perceive the need for a preemptive strike. But I have absolutely no idea how to go about it. If we knew how, or where, William and his accomplice were finding their victims, I could go there and make myself conspicuous."

"Not even the police have been able to figure that out," Paige said somberly. "Aside from their physical strength, the victims don't seem to have anything at all in common."

"Except that they're all human," Piper put in.

"Which doesn't get us all that far," Phoebe added somewhat glumly.

"Wait a minute," Lucile said suddenly. "This may seem terribly old-fashioned, but when I was a schoolgirl, we were taught that all humans, no matter their social differences, always have at least two fundamental things in common: the need for food and the need for shelter. What if it's something as basic as that?"

"You know," Piper said slowly, "Lucile just might have a point. It was when we concentrated on what might be the basic motivational factors—love, hate, and revenge—that we finally made a breakthrough before."

"So what's William's henchman doing, cruising real estate offices?" Paige asked.

"Not enough variety," Phoebe said at once. "Which leaves us with food. My bet is he's going to the grocery store."

"Okay, I'll buy that," Paige said. "The question is, which one?"

"Most likely it's more than one," Piper said as she, too, entered into the spirit of the chase. "But they have to have a home base, where they're keeping William's body. Could he stick close to home because of that, then follow his victims to wherever they lived?"

"Maybe," Phoebe said slowly. "But most people tend to shop in their own neighborhood, don't they? The victims are all over town."

"But people run errands all over the place," Paige countered. "How many times have we headed off somewhere, discovered we've forgotten something, and stopped at the next store we saw?"

"Often enough," Phoebe said. "But I still think—"

"There's a grocery store about three blocks from Mural House, isn't there?" Lucile suddenly inquired. "One that went in just a couple of years ago? I remember because the location caused a big zoning fight. As a property owner in the neighborhood, I got all sorts of information from both sides."

"That's right, there is!" Phoebe exclaimed. "Paige and I drove right by it the night we attended the gala."

"So why not try there?" Lucile asked. "There's another basic here—or maybe I should say, a constant. And that's Mural House. It's where this whole thing started."

"That's a good point," Piper acknowledged. "How about we divide and conquer? Phoebes, you go to work and tackle your desk. Paige can stay here and work on Donovan Hawthorne's background. Meanwhile, Lucile, Wyatt, and I will take a field trip to the grocery store."

"I have just one question," Lucile said.

"Okay," Piper said. "That's entirely reasonable. What is it?"

"Can I push the cart?"

He had found her.

He could hardly believe the unexpectedness of it. The exhilaration of his discovery still coursed through his veins, more potent than any wine.

She'd slipped through his fingers once, the day she'd left the hospital. When he'd been unable to trace her, his fury had known no bounds. Fury with her, but also with himself. She was old; she was a woman. A combination that should have made her easy to defeat. Instead, she had confounded him. Made him look like a fool. Worse than that, she'd threatened to undo everything. To ruin everything.

He supposed he shouldn't have been surprised. She was her mother's daughter, after all.

But now he had found her, had seen her when she hadn't seen him, and all would be well. The final piece had fallen into place. Now he had only to do what must be done. One final task, and it would all be over. His life's work complete.

All it would take was the death of one old woman.

"That's 'Amazing Grace,' isn't it?" the young woman behind the checkout counter asked as she ran the bag of chips he'd selected at random across the scanner.

"What?" he said.

"That tune you're humming. It's called 'Amazing Grace.'"

He flashed a smile, the one he'd learned people would remember instead of the details of his face.

"That's right, it is."

"It's one of my favorites," she said. "And you have a lovely singing voice." A sudden blush swept over her features. "I bet people are always telling you that."

"No, not at all," he said. "But even if they did, it's not the sort of thing I'd mind hearing again."

He let his smile get a little wider as he scooped up the shopping bag.

"'I once was lost, but now am found.' That's my favorite part," the checkout girl confided.

"You know what? Mine too," he said.

Chapter Eighteen

"How are things going?" Phoebe asked as soon as Paige answered the phone at Halliwell Manor.

"So far, so good. Not that anybody has much to show for it," Paige replied. She tucked the portable phone against one shoulder while her hands continued to work the keyboard of her laptop. "Researching Donovan Hawthorne is sort of like waiting for spring to come. You know something's bound to happen, sooner or later. It just takes way too long.

"About a year after the vandalism of Miranda Nance's artwork stopped, believe it or not, Donovan resurfaced in San Francisco. I know this because he got married to a woman named Claire Emerson."

"Somebody actually married that guy?" Phoebe's voice exclaimed in Paige's ear. "Talk about smart women making poor choices."

"Either that, or she wasn't all that smart to

start out with," Paige remarked. "Anyhow. The marriage didn't last very long. Because approximately nine months later, Claire dies in childbirth and Donovan and the baby drop out of sight. That's where the trail ends. After Claire's death, there's absolutely no record of Donovan Hawthorne."

"That can't be right," Phoebe said.

"I'm going to take a break, give the little gray cells a rest, then tackle this puzzle again after lunch," Paige answered. "Donovan has to have gone somewhere. I just have to figure out how he covered his snaky tracks."

"Lucile and Piper back from the grocery store yet?" Phoebe inquired.

"Just a little while ago," Paige confirmed.

"And?"

"Nothing, which I'm thinking is both good news and bad," Paige said. "The good news is, they're home safe and sound. But I think Lucile is genuinely disappointed nothing happened. She really wants to help."

"The best way for her to do that is to stay alive," Phoebe remarked. "Speaking of which . . ."

"You got something?" Paige asked. She sat up straighter in the chair and turned away from the keyboard.

"To tell you the truth, I'm not quite sure," Phoebe acknowledged. "There was this letter on my desk when I got in this morning. It was pretty well toward the bottom of this enormous stack of mail, which explains why I'm just getting to it now. In it, a woman named . . ."

Through the phone, Paige could hear the sound of paper being shuffled. ". . . Jennifer Bowman describes recent changes in her relationship with her boyfriend, Seymour."

"There are guys out there named Seymour?" Paige asked.

"Apparently," Phoebe answered, "there is at least one. The problem is that this particular Seymour seems to have undergone a personality transplant. I'm quoting from Jennifer's letter now:

At first we were the perfect couple. I couldn't believe how much we had in common. Sooner or later, all the other guys I'd ever gone out with ended up being more interested in themselves than in a relationship. It wasn't that way with Seymour.

Then things changed, and the really weird thing is that it's almost like it happened overnight. One day, he was supportive and interested in my opinions. The next, he suddenly starts this big fight. Out of nowhere, he's yelling at me about how selfish I am. How I'm not interested in what he wants anymore. I'm only interested in myself. When I got to the part in Isabella's letters where she talks about how William changed, how unhappy and confused that made her, it's like I was reading about myself.

One day, Seymour was the man I loved.
The next day, he'd turned into someone else.

"Oh, wow," Paige said. "Personality transplant is right. And I think I see exactly where you're going. You're thinking it's too much of a coincidence, a guy suddenly behaving just like William did? You're thinking William might actually be involved?"

"I'm thinking it might be worth checking into," Phoebe said. "This letter's probably been on my desk for about a week, well within the time frame of when we now know William's mind has been free to wander around. Maybe he's, I don't know, mind-hopping, flexing his mental muscles.

"I'd go check this out myself, if I could. But I'm just starting to make a dent in all of the work here."

"It's okay," Paige said. "I'd be glad to have a break and do something that feels constructive. What's the address?"

Quickly, she jotted down the information Phoebe provided.

"I was hoping you'd say yes, so I took the liberty of phoning ahead. She's expecting you," Phoebe confided. "I said I was sending over someone from my office. The paper wants to do some follow-ups with readers whose own letters seem particularly connected to William and Isabella's story. When you get there, just get the best sense you can of what's going on. Take your cell with you. Stay in touch."

"Will do," Paige said. "And I'll update Piper on my way out."

"Right," Phoebe concurred. "Thanks, Paige. I really appreciate this. Good luck."

We need more than that, Paige thought. What the Charmed Ones needed was a lead that actually went somewhere.

Maybe, at last, Phoebe had found one.

"I'm sorry to have to call you at home like this, Piper."

"That's okay, Gil," Piper said. "It pretty much comes with the owner territory."

With a gesture of her head, which was about her only unemcumbered body part, she requested backup from Lucile, who quickly hurried across the kitchen to take Wyatt out of her arms. They settled in at the kitchen table, Wyatt on Lucile's lap. Piper gave her full attention to the phone. The call had come just moments after Paige had departed on her errand for Phoebe.

"What's going on? Are you at the club?" Piper asked now.

"I am," Gil confirmed. "I'm not on for hours yet, of course. But I was in the neighborhood, so I just sort of dropped by. That's when I found him."

"Found who?" Piper said. "Gil, you're not making any sense. Is somebody hurt? What's wrong?"

"He's not hurt badly," Gil said quickly.

Piper felt her pulse boost up a notch. "*Who's* not hurt badly?" she demanded.

"I don't actually know his name," Gil admitted. "I found him out behind the club. He'd slipped and fallen in the alley. It's been kind of damp—you know how it gets when it's this foggy. It's just wet pavement. A thing like this could have happened anywhere. The trouble is, this guy's insisting it's P3's fault."

"Oh, for crying out loud!" Piper exclaimed. "That's nonsense."

"You know that, and I know that," Gil said. "But, so far, we're the only ones. He's an older gentleman—did I mention that? To tell you the truth"—Gil's voice dropped to a whisper—"I'm not entirely certain he's still got all his marbles. When he found out I was the club manager, he demanded I call the owner at once. If you don't come down here in person, he says he's going to sue."

"Which means he'll probably sue anyhow, or he wants some sort of payoff not to," Piper said. "Threats. You gotta love 'em."

"I hate to sound like an idiot, but I didn't know what else to do," Gil said, speaking in his regular tone. "It did seem like a situation you'd want to know about, so I went ahead and placed the call."

"You did exactly right," Piper said at once. "And of course I'll be right down. Though if this guy thinks he can steamroller me, he's got another think coming."

"I can't tell you how much I'm looking forward to watching you say that to him in person," Gil said.

"Right," Piper snorted. "Make our mystery guest as comfortable as you can, Gil. I'll be right down."

"Thanks, Piper."

"Oh, dear," Piper exclaimed as she punched the off button on the portable phone. She placed the unit back into the charger with an irritated slap.

"Something wrong?" Lucile inquired.

"An older gentleman slipped and fell in the alley behind P3, my club," Piper explained. "According to my manager, who was passing by, the guy is busy claiming it's the club's fault. He's demanding to see me in person and threatening to sue. I'm afraid I'm going to have to go down there."

"I'll get Wyatt ready," Lucile said at once. "I think it's better if we stay together, don't you?"

"I do," Piper acknowledged. "You're sure you don't mind?"

"Only when you ask silly questions like that," Lucile responded as she stood up. "You might want to contact your own lawyer while Wyatt and I get ready," she advised as she headed for the kitchen door. "And if you don't already have one, go look up one with an impressive-sounding name so you can hit this guy with it the minute you walk in the door. If this is a scam, that ought to give him pause."

"The best defense is a strong offense," Piper said.

"Precisely," Lucile replied. "Just give us a minute."

Still holding Wyatt, she bustled off. Deciding to take Lucile's advice, Piper turned back to the phone. She put in a call to the family lawyer but declined his offer to accompany her to the club. Though she wouldn't hesitate to call him in if his services really did become necessary, initially Piper was going to aim for a more low-key approach. Then she quickly called Phoebe to let her know about the trip to P3.

"All set," Lucile announced as she and Wyatt returned. Lucile was wearing a light jacket against the fog that had been been dampening the city all morning. Wyatt was wearing a brand-new sweatshirt with 49ERS emblazoned on the front.

"That's another new shirt," Piper accused. "Lucile, you're going to spoil him."

"That's the plan," Lucile said cheerfully as she and Piper headed for the front door. "He'll get spoiled, you'll get tired and want a break, then I'll be forced to come over and babysit."

"Very clever," Piper said as she pulled on a lightweight coat. "I'm thinking it just might work."

"You hear that, Wyatt? We're all set," Lucile whispered in a stage voice.

In spite of her annoyance with the errand they were about to run, Piper smiled all the way to the car.

Chapter Nineteen

"So what he did was, he took her name. Can you believe that?"

"First time I've ever heard of it. Hey, Phoebe. How's it going?"

"Fine, thanks, Elaine," Phoebe said.

Deciding that she needed a break from the stacks still covering her desk, Phoebe had ducked into the break room at the paper for a quick, heavily caffeinated soda. If that didn't speed up her afternoon, she didn't know what would. She'd gone halfway back across the room when the conversation between Elaine—who worked on the section that included both obituaries and wedding announcements—and a coworker whose name Phoebe didn't know had ensnared her attention.

"Not to eavesdrop or anything," she went on now.

"Oh, that's all right. It's hardly a secret," Elaine

said with a wave of her hand. "I was just telling Joanna about this wedding announcement that just came in. The guy took the girl's last name. Can you believe that?"

"Hmmm," Phoebe said.

"It was actually kind of sweet," Elaine went on. "You know how some announcements include family info? Well, apparently this guy lost most of his family at an early age, but he's close to his wife's parents. So, to show how happy he is to officially be a member of their family, he's taking his wife's last name. He's getting the family he always wanted, and they're getting a son to carry on the family name."

"That is sweet," Phoebe said. She could almost feel her mind shoot straight into high gear, a thing that had absolutely nothing to do with her high-caffeine soda. "Thanks for filling me in. See you later. The desk calls."

"I hear that," Elaine said.

Quickly, Phoebe left the break room and headed back for her office. Once there, she rooted through the papers on her desk until she located the one onto which she'd spontaneously jotted down the notes she'd taken of her conversation with Paige earlier that day.

There it is, she thought. And there was the name of the woman Donovan Hawthorne had married. The woman who'd delivered him a son, then conveniently died. Claire Emerson.

It might take a minute or two to confirm, but

unless Phoebe entirely missed her guess, she had just figured out how Donovan Hawthorne had managed to drop off the radar.

By hiding in plain sight.

"It's about time!"

The voice was the first that Piper heard as she walked through the doors of P3 with Wyatt in her arms. A voice that somehow managed to be petulant and aggressive at the same time. After just three words, she could see why Gil had been so quick to call for reinforcements.

I'd have done the same thing, she thought. Not only that, she could also imagine perfectly how P3's mystery guest had come to fall. The day was thick and misty with fog, making the roads and sidewalks slick. It was the reason she, not Lucile, was carrying Wyatt. She wanted the older woman to have her hands free.

"Well, I'm here now," Piper said as she moved into the club. Though the bar was lit, as if Gil had been working while awaiting her arrival, the rest of the club was dim. Piper could make out a figure on the edge of the table-seating area.

"Gil?"

"Here, Piper," Gil's voice sounded.

"Why don't you turn on a few more lights?" she called.

"Because I asked him not to," the old man's voice snapped. "I don't like bright lights. They hurt my eyes. I've already been injured once today. I see no reason to subject myself to any additional discomfort."

"The regular club lights are all on dimmers," Piper said firmly yet quietly as she continued toward him. "Gil, please turn them on, but keep them down low."

It was definitely time to establish who was in control around here, she thought. Not to mention getting to the bottom of what was going on.

"I'm sorry to hear of your accident," Piper said. "Mr.—" She paused. When no name was forthcoming, she continued. "Perhaps you'd care to tell me how it happened."

Around her, with almost theatrical slowness, the level of the lights in the club began to rise.

"How it happened," the petulant voice echoed. "I'll tell you how it happened. I was betrayed by a treacherous woman."

"No!"

The single syllable, uttered in Lucile's voice, had Piper halting, dead in her tracks, just as the lights became bright enough for her to finally get a good look at the man in front of her.

He looked like something out of an old horror film. *The Phantom of the Nightclub,* Piper thought. He wasn't sitting in one of her club chairs, as she'd originally thought, but in a wheelchair. His body was a strange, ruined combination of old crumbling into young. The legs looked withered and useless, but the arms were clearly strong.

And it was never static. The body in front of

her was changing from moment to moment as
Piper watched. One minute the face was so
handsome, it all but took Piper's breath away.
The next, it was shriveled and shrunken. Only
the eyes remained constant. A fierce and cun-
ning green, burning brightly as some bizarre
springtime version of the fires of hell.

"William Lancaster, I presume?"

"You found out what?" Paige yelped. Her meeting with Jennifer wrapped, Paige had been
heading for the nearest coffee bar when her cell
phone had gone off. Quickly, she'd picked up.

"I found out what happened to Donovan
Hawthorne," Phoebe said. "I know how he
dropped from sight."

"I'm glad you got somewhere," Paige said.
"Jennifer and Seymour were a big dead end."

"That doesn't matter anymore," Phoebe said.
Quickly, she related what the conversation she'd
had in the paper's break room had enabled her
to accomplish.

"When his wife died, Donovan took her last
name, a pattern that was later repeated by his
son."

"Convenient the way they got the women out
of the picture, wouldn't you say?" Paige commented as she felt a chill snake down her spine
that had nothing to do with the San Francisco
fog.

"Definitely," Phoebe said. "But that's not the

creepiest part. I'll give you two guesses what last name Donovan's grandson inherited."

Paige stopped walking. "Wait a minute. Don't tell me," she said. "Omigod. That guy. The new guy. Piper's new manager."

"You got it. The last name of Donovan Hawthorne's grandson is Townsend."

"Gil," Piper said calmly. "I'd like you to call the police. Right now."

"I'm sorry. I'm afraid I can't do that, Piper," Gil said. With his easy stride, he moved to stand beside the figure in the wheelchair. Behind her, Piper heard Lucile give a low moan.

"Donovan," she said. "Donovan Hawthorne."

"Not precisely," Gil said simply. "But it's an entirely understandable mistake. My father always said the family resemblance was very strong. Donovan Hawthorne was my grandfather."

"Lucile," Piper said, striving to keep her own voice calm. Slowly, her eyes still on Gil and William, Piper turned toward the older woman, standing just behind her. "Please take Wyatt."

Let me free my hands! she thought. Once Piper had the unencumbered use of her hands, she could end the situation in a moment. With one gesture, she could freeze William and Gil, then phone her sisters and the police herself. Lucile would be safe. The murders at an end.

She extended her arms, holding Wyatt firmly

between her hands. "Lucile," she said, her tone more urgent this time.

Unexpectedly, she felt Lucile's fingers wrap—and hold tight—around her wrists. Startled, Piper finally turned her gaze away from Gil and William and looked into Lucile Marshall's horrified eyes.

Lucile's whole body shook, as if she were standing in the freezing cold. Her mouth worked, snapping open, then shut, as if struggling in some internal argument with itself. Her eyes, terrified and furious, stared straight into Piper's own.

"I'm afraid she won't be able to help you, either," Gil Townsend said. He moved to Piper's side. With one quick gesture, he plucked Wyatt from her captive hands and shoved him into Lucile's arms.

"But you'll forgive her, won't you?" he asked sweetly. "The truth is, she's not quite herself at the moment."

"Okay," Paige said. "I'm on my way home."

"No, wait!" Phoebe cried. "Going home won't do any good. Piper phoned me just after you left. She got a call from the club."

"Uh-oh," Paige said.

"You're not kidding," Phoebe said. "I'm in a cab, and I'm almost there now."

"On my way," Paige said. "You want me to take the fast way, or the fast way?"

"Yes," Phoebe replied.

• • •

"You can still stop this," Piper said, then winced as Gil jerked on the hands he was tying behind her back.

There's a horrible irony here somewhere, Piper thought.

Gil had absolutely no idea that in tying her hands behind her, he'd incapacitated a magic at least as strong as the one that had held William Lancaster a prisoner for more than eighty years. Instead, he was simply taking care of the only person who might able to protect Lucile in the most straightforward way possible.

"It's not too late. Think about what you're doing, Gil."

Gil tightened Piper's bonds, then checked to make sure they were secure before he spoke.

"What makes you think I haven't thought about it? Helping William is my life's work, just as it was my father's and my grandfather's. It's all I think about, Piper."

"How can you help him?" Piper asked. "He's a monster."

"That's a lie," William Lancaster croaked.

"No, it's not," Lucile said suddenly. They were her first words since William had released her mind. He'd been beside himself with glee at the success of his unexpected ploy, chortling and gloating while Gil had tied Piper up and Lucile had stood, helpless and stricken, with Wyatt in her arms. The sound had grated on

Piper's nerves like fingernails along a blackboard.

"I remember," Lucile went on. "I remember what you did to my mother. You tried to destroy her. She loved you."

"She didn't love me!" William screamed. "She never truly loved me. If she had, she'd have given me what I wanted. That's what true love is."

"I never thought I'd say this, William Lancaster," Lucile said quietly. "But I feel sorry for you. You ruined your own life. You ruined my mother's. And all for something you don't understand at all."

"Save your pity for yourself, old woman," William said, his tone bitter and filled with loathing. "In a few minutes you'll be dead, and I'll be eating your beating heart."

"I don't think so, pal."

"Phoebe!" Piper cried.

She had no idea what had brought her sister here at precisely the moment she needed her most. Not that it mattered. She was more than happy to chalk it up to the Power of Three. Unseen, but never unimportant.

"Don't forget about me," another voice suddenly chimed in. Piper felt a huge wave of relief sweep through her as Paige orbed into view beside Lucile and Wyatt. "Back in a flash," Paige said as she wrapped her arms around them. She looked over at Gil, standing transfixed beside William Lancaster.

"Though you don't have wait around for me before you start busting his ass, Phoebes."

"Thanks. I don't intend to," Phoebe answered with a grim smile.

"This is going to seem a little unusual, Lucile," Paige said. "Sometimes it helps if you close your eyes."

"If it means Wyatt will be safe, I'm up for it," Lucile answered.

"Excellent," Paige said. "Home!" she pronounced. In a shower of glittering sparks, she, Wyatt, and Lucile orbed out.

Gil Townsend's jaw dropped open.

"No!" William Lancaster roared. He struggled to rise from his chair, but his legs refused to hold him. "We have to get her back. We must complete the spell."

"It's all right, William. I'll take care of things," Gil said. "Don't tax your strength. You must stay calm."

He glanced toward Piper, his eyes narrowed. Any trace of the friendly, easygoing Gil Townsend she thought she'd known was now completely gone. As Piper watched, Gil, his movements unhurried, unzipped the backpack hanging from the handle of William's wheelchair.

"Phoebe, watch out," Piper suddenly called out. "He's got a knife."

"Not just any knife," Gil said. "An athame. One sacrifice may have slipped through our hands, but I think I know where I can find another option. The friend of my enemy is my enemy. I think that means you'll do just fine."

He took a step toward Piper.

"Some men you two are," Phoebe taunted. Slowly, knees bent and feet firmly planted, she began to move closer. "What's the matter? Afraid to take on someone who's not a member of AARP or all tied up?"

Oh, good girl, Phoebe, Piper thought. When in doubt, go for the male ego. It was almost always a vulnerable spot.

"I took you down once," Phoebe went on. She was closer, almost within Gil's striking distance now. At the first sound of Phoebe's voice, Gil had frozen in place, his body still turned toward Piper. But he followed Phoebe's every movement with his eyes.

"How much you wanna bet I can do it a second time?"

Still, Gil stayed motionless. Piper could almost hear the thoughts racing through his mind. Just a few steps would take him to where she sat, completely defenseless. But to do that would be to refuse Phoebe's challenge.

"You're going to make me do it, aren't you?" Phoebe said as if she, too, were taking stock of the conflict in Gil Townsend's mind. What she needed was the thing that would push him over the edge. "You're going to make me use the *c* word. That's all right. I don't mind."

"I know what you're trying to do," Gil rasped

out. "I can see right through you. It's not going to work."

"Chicken," Phoebe chanted softly.

With a roar of rage, knife held high, Gil launched himself toward her. At the exact same moment, Phoebe threw herself forward. Her momentum caused Gil to overshoot the mark. Rolling as gracefully as if she were on a practice mat instead of a hard floor, Phoebe completed her move, then spun around. The two combatants faced each other, then began to circle.

"Hang on just a sec, Piper," a voice suddenly whispered in her ear. "I'll have you out of these in no time."

"Boy, am I glad to see you," Piper whispered back as she caught the telltale sparkle of Paige's orb transit out of the corner of her eye. "For the second time. Lucile and Wyatt safe?"

"Safe and sound at home," Paige said. "Lucile's calling the police even as we speak. She didn't make a peep about the whole orb thing. That lady definitely has guts."

Piper felt her bonds loosen. "Hurry," she urged, her eyes on the fight.

"There!" Paige cried just as Gil lunged toward Phoebe again. As she moved to respond, William intervened. Careening his wheelchair into Phoebe's legs, he knocked her down, then continued straight toward Piper. With a cry of triumph, Gil leaped at Phoebe, brandishing the knife.

Piper whipped her arms out from behind her

back. Gil and William froze. Gil's knife was just inches from Phoebe's chest.

"Thanks," she said as she slowly eased herself out from under it. She got to her feet. "Talk about the nick of time."

"I'd rather not," Piper said simply. "I'm thinking it cuts a little too close to home."

"Ouch," Paige said. "So, what do we do now?"

"I'd suggest giving Mr. Mind Over Matter a taste of his own medicine," Phoebe said.

"I second that notion," Piper replied.

"Can you do a little selective unfreezing?" Paige asked.

Piper considered a moment. "I think so. Let's get the mind-meld thing in place first."

"Hey," Phoebe protested. "I wanted to be the one to say that."

Piper smiled. "You do the spell. After all, it's mostly your fight."

"Okay," Phoebe said. She pulled in a breath, then extended both hands. Piper and Paige each took one, then clasped hands themselves. The Charmed Ones now formed a perfect circle, a living embodiment of the Power of Three.

"Focus in the center of the circle," Phoebe said. "Visualize our thoughts becoming one. I'm thinking a ball of white light."

"Like Glinda the Good Witch," Paige put in.

"Okay by me," Phoebe said. "Everybody ready? Here we go."

She began the spell.

Powers of balance, powers of light.
Help us now to make things right.
Join our minds in harmony.
Let all bear the strength of three.

In front of her, in the center of the circle, Piper could see a ball of clear, white light begin to form. Her mind felt flooded by its brilliance. She could hear her sisters' thoughts as clearly as her own.

"All set?" Phoebe asked.

"Set," Piper replied.

Slowly, as each sister put her will to the task, the light began to rise. It hovered in the air above their heads, then moved to where William Lancaster sat motionless, trapped in time. It hung above his head for a moment, then began to settle down. The second the sphere of light touched William's head, Piper let go of Phoebe's hand. With one quick gesture, she unfroze William.

As she broke contact with Phoebe, severing the circle, Piper felt a brief dimming of the light in her mind. Then she and her sisters were clasping hands once more. Not in a circle, this time, but in a line, facing William Lancaster.

As William felt the Charmed Ones' thoughts entering his mind, he gave a great cry. His strong arms gripped the chair. His head snaked from side to side.

"No," he gasped out. "I won't do it. You can't make me. I'm still stronger than you are."

Phoebe began to chant once more.

Powers of balance, pure and strong,
Help us now to right a wrong.
Vanquish evil, set goodness free.
As we will, so mote it be.

William's arms spasmed. He flung his body from side to side. His hands gripped the wheels of his chair so tightly the tendons stood out. Then, his body still straining, William Lancaster began to turn himself around. His harsh gasps were the only sound in the room as he finally understood what it truly meant for one person to be controlled by another.

Slowly, inexorably, William pushed himself across the room until it was his chest, not Phoebe's, that lay unprotected beneath Gil Townsend's sacrificial knife.

"Ready to release?" Phoebe asked.

"Ready," Piper said.

"Now!" Phoebe cried.

The Charmed Ones broke contact at the exact same moment, releasing William from the mind-control spell. In one quick, fluid gesture, Piper brought her hands up, freeing Gil from his entrapment in time. His forward momentum was impossible to stop. The athame, the sacrificial knife, flashed down. Gil staggered back, staring in horror at the hilt, which now protruded from William's chest.

"William," he choked out. He fell to his knees

beside the older man. "Forgive me. What have I done?"

"Peace," William Lancaster said after a moment. His eyes closed, then opened once more. "You have given me peace. I thank you for it."

Then his eyelids drooped. His eyes stayed closed. Over the sound of Gil's heartbroken sobbing, Piper heard the wail of sirens.

Chapter Twenty

"Thank you for meeting me here, my dear," Lucile said.

"My pleasure," Phoebe responded. "It does seem right, somehow."

"I knew you'd understand," Lucile said. "I just felt . . . before I could move on."

"You don't have to explain it to me," Phoebe said. "Shall we go up?"

"By all means," Lucile said.

Together, as they had done just a few weeks ago, the two women climbed the stairs of Mural House.

It was Lucile who had suggested that she and Phoebe rendezvous here. They hadn't seen much of each other in the weeks since the murders had been solved. Most of the details would never be released to the public. Gil Townsend would never come to trial. William Lancaster's death had completely unhinged his mind.

Though he'd been raving, hysterical when the police had arrived at P3, not long afterward Gil had fallen into a state that was even more disturbing. He was completely catatonic, unresponsive to outside stimuli.

It was as if, without the framework of William's will, his desires, Gil Townsend had simply ceased to have a mind at all. But Phoebe had never forgotten William's final words. In releasing him from life, Gil had brought William peace. It seemed the words of her spell, to vanquish evil and set goodness free, had been more prophetic than she could have known.

And it meant that Lucile had been right about William Lancaster. He hadn't started out evil. He'd simply been all too human, all too corruptible.

"What do you think?" she asked now.

Lucile was silent for a moment. The two women had climbed the stairs and reached their destination: William's full-length portrait.

"I think you're right," Lucile finally replied. "He looks at peace. And I think . . . I'm glad of it. If he's at peace, perhaps Mama and Miranda are too."

She gave Phoebe's shoulders a quick, hard squeeze. "Thank you, my dear," she said simply. "I don't think it could have happened without you and your sisters."

"Lucile," Phoebe said. "About that day at the club."

But Lucile was already shaking her head. "I've said I don't want any explanation, and I mean that, Phoebe," she said. "It's not that I'm not curious, of course. But it's also not as if I can't figure some things out for myself. My own experiences as a child showed me that certain kinds of power really do exist. Surely if I accept that, I must also accept that there are those who wield that power. I don't need to know the ins and outs of how you and your sisters do what you do. How or why, or even what, you are what you are. It's enough for me to know that you exist. And I will never forget what you have done."

"You really are remarkable," Phoebe said.

"Yes," Lucile answered. "But do you still think I'm terrifying?"

"Absolutely," Phoebe replied.

"That's all right, then," Lucile said. "Now, let's go somewhere incredibly expensive, eat fattening pastries, and drink strong coffee. I want you to help me decide where to go on my trip. I've decided it's time for me to see the world. From now on, I want the pictures on the walls of my apartment to be ones I take myself."

"I'd love to," Phoebe said.

Together, the two women left Mural House and went out into the bright San Francisco sunshine.

As many as 1 in 3 Americans
who have HIV... don't know it.

TAKE CONTROL.
KNOW YOUR STATUS.
GET TESTED.

To learn more about HIV testing,
or get a free guide to HIV and
other sexually transmitted diseases:

www.knowhivaids.org
1-866-344-KNOW

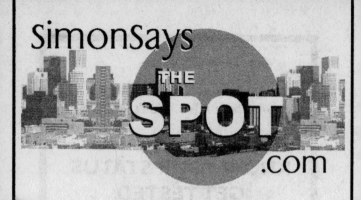